THE
SPIRIT
GIRLS

Happy reading
and God bless!

THE
SPIRIT
GIRLS

DAWN
MERRIMAN

SECOND SKY

Published by Second Sky in 2023

An imprint of Storyfire Ltd.
Carmelite House
50 Victoria Embankment
London EC4Y 0DZ
United Kingdom

www.secondskybooks.com

ISBN: 978-1-83790-403-7
eBook ISBN: 978-1-83790-402-0

This book is dedicated to my husband, Kevin.
Thank you for all your help and your constant support.

ONE

RYLAN FLYNN

I should be afraid, but I'm not. The shadow figure stands at the end of the hall, her face turned away from me. The exit sign above her glows red in the moonlight. Doors line the hallway, leading to patient rooms in the abandoned hospital. One of them slams shut; no one is near it. Dust sifts down from the ceiling, and the sound echoes through the old building.

"I know you're upset, but we are not here to hurt you," I tell the figure. Another door slams and the figure moves closer. No feet are visible, but I can hear the footsteps.

Behind me, I hear Mickey, my assistant with the camera, gasp as the shadow looms close to my face.

"I can hear the steps," she whispers.

"She's right in front of me," I tell her. "Keep filming."

A hand reaches for my face. Every instinct tells me I should be terrified, but I'm more curious.

"What do you need?" I ask the figure.

The woman's face peeks out behind long hair. The mouth is drawn and the eyes are dark. She touches my face and my skin grows cold.

"You can see me?" she asks.

I nod, fighting the urge to pull my face away. I don't want to startle her or she will disappear.

"This place, it isn't nice like they said it would be." Her voice is so full of sorrow, it nearly breaks my heart. In my line of work, they are always sad stories. Those with happy endings don't stick around for me to see.

"I'm so sorry you went through that," I tell her.

The ghost drops her hand and turns away. "Nothing to do about it now."

"I can help you leave here," I call after her.

She turns and pushes her hair back, revealing the slice in her throat. I try not to flinch, but she sees the shift in my expression.

"Now you see. I did this." She points to her neck. "If I leave here, I don't want to see where I'll go."

"I can help you," I repeat.

"Silly girl, I'm beyond help."

She flicks her wrist and another door slams. This time, I jump at the sound, making my charm bracelet jangle.

The woman disappears into the shadows again.

"Did you get all that?" I ask Mickey, breathless from the encounter.

"I got your side of the conversation. And the doors slamming, of course. Try moving over toward that door that just closed. Yeah, right there."

I take a breath. I sometimes forget that I'm the only one that can see them. Putting on a smile, I turn toward the camera. "This is Rylan Flynn with *Beyond the Dead Investigations*. I just had the most amazing encounter."

A crash from the first floor of the hospital interrupts my sign-off.

"Rylan? Are you up there?"

I sigh, recognizing the voice shouting my name as Officer Frazier of the Ashby, Indiana, police department. He is not a fan of our YouTube show.

Mickey lowers the camera. "Busted."

"Frazier, you ruined the shot," I shout through the hospital corridor, my voice echoing down the stairs.

Real footsteps storm closer as Officer Frazier comes round the corner. I half expect him to be holding his gun, but he only has a flashlight. It is bright in my eyes. I can't see his face, but I'm sure he is fuming.

"When I got the call that someone was snooping around this old place, I knew it would be you two. Filming again? You know you can't trespass here."

"She actually talked to her tonight," Mickey gushes.

Frazier turns his light on Mickey, then snaps back in my direction. I hold up a hand to the piercing beam. "Can you put that thing away? There's plenty of moonlight in here."

He switches the flashlight off and dark spots dance in my vision. "Did you really talk to the Morton Mistress?" The sarcasm is heavy when he says the name of the legendary ghost that haunts the Morton Mental Hospital on the edge of Ashby. "I'm sure your viewers will fall for this hoax, but I won't."

"It's not a hoax," Mickey says. "She really did. I saw it."

"You saw the ghost?" he asks her.

"Well, no. But I heard her footsteps. And she slammed the doors."

"Uh-huh." There's not a sliver of belief in his voice. "Keep telling yourself that. Now, get your camera and get out of here before I haul you in for trespassing."

Mickey huffs. "She really saw her."

I put a hand on my friend's arm. "It's okay, Mickey. If Officer Frazier doesn't believe, that is his problem."

"But you talked to her. I saw it."

Frazier's glare is sharp, even in the darkness.

"I know. Come on, let's get out of here." I follow Mickey

down the dark stairs, Frazier so close behind me I can smell his cloying cologne.

I'm thankful for the fresh air as we exit the heavy doors. Huge trees sway on the wide front lawn, dancing in the moonlight. We step out under a canopy of stars.

"They really need to lock this place up," Frazier says, as he makes sure the door is shut tight behind us.

"That won't keep her out." The deep voice from the dark sidewalk makes my heart beat faster. I'd recognize it anywhere.

Ford Pierce, Ashby's head detective, steps from the shadow of a tree. The sight of him makes me tingle, but I push that down.

"What are you doing here?" I demand. "Does it take the whole Ashby police force to chase two women out of an abandoned building?"

"I heard the call on the radio and figured I'd come remind you myself that you can't be in here."

"Frazier already made that abundantly clear." I wish my heart would slow down, but Ford has me flustered. Running a hand down my long brown hair, I find a cobweb is caught in it. I shake the cobweb from my hand, feeling ridiculous. "What if I get a permit?"

"I don't think that will happen. No one wants you poking around here looking for something that doesn't exist. It's dangerous in there. You could get hurt. Besides, the Morton Mistress is a legend, Rylan, that's all." I melt when he says my name, but lift my chin in defiance.

"I talked to her tonight."

There's a flicker of surprise in his blue eyes. "Really?"

"She did," Mickey pipes in. "Wait until you see the video."

Ford shakes his head. "The Morton Mistress is a story to scare little kids."

I'm secretly hurt that he doesn't believe me. Ever since we were children, and he came over to play with my brother,

Keaton, Ford's opinion has mattered. I don't let him see that now. "Believe what you want." I toss my brown hair over my shoulder and walk past him. "Come on, Mickey. We have an episode to edit."

Mickey follows me down the sidewalk to the old tan Cadillac I inherited from my mom.

"You won't come back, right?" Frazier calls into the parking lot.

"Don't worry. I got what I needed," I say over the hood of my car. Mickey carefully puts the camera in the backseat, then climbs in the passenger side.

I open my door and slide in next to her. I try to fight the urge to look in the rearview mirror for a last view of Ford.

I lose the battle.

Holy flip, he looks good, even while shaking his head at me.

TWO

RYLAN FLYNN

We pull away from the old hospital and drive down the tree-lined lane, through the brick and wrought-iron gates. Mickey looks at the camera in the backseat. "That was some great footage. I can't wait to edit it."

"You think?"

"Once I get it edited and do the voiceovers, it's going to be great. The viewers will love it."

I'm keyed up after the encounter and seeing Ford. I leave the show-making details to Mickey and turn up the radio. I tap my hand against the steering wheel to the Panic! At the Disco song, "Nicotine." After jamming out I feel more centered.

I think of the Morton Mistress and how sad she seemed. "The poor thing. It looks like she cut her throat and died. She's worried she won't go to the good side now."

"Maybe your dad can talk to her, explain it all. That would be amazing to get on film."

"I'll ask him about the best way to help her after his sermon on Sunday. In the meantime, wow, what an episode this will make."

Mickey sings along to the next song for a few bars. I turn up the music and join her. We belt out the lyrics. The singing is a tradition after a sighting, a way to get out the buildup of emotion it entails. When I see a ghost, I often feel their feelings. It can be exhilarating, but also exhausting. My singing is interrupted by a huge yawn.

"Phew, that one kind of wiped me out," I say when the song is over.

"Let's edit it tomorrow, after you've gotten some rest," Mickey says.

I yawn again, making Mickey yawn, too. We giggle like girls at that. "I have breakfast with Aunt Val in the morning, but I can do it after."

I turn down Mickey's street and pull the Caddy to a stop in front of her house. Large tree branches hang into the street, sending shadows over the car. A light is on inside her house, a welcoming sight in the dark of night.

"Sweet, looks like Marco's home early." Mickey is a newlywed whose husband works late most nights. She hurries to get the camera out of the backseat and says goodbye. Before I can respond, she closes the door and scurries up the walk, obviously excited for a few extra hours with Marco.

I watch her with a tinge of jealousy. At twenty-eight, I'm at the age where most of my friends are either married with kids or headed that way soon. I have barely dated. Sometimes I tell myself that the problem is most people in Ashby know that I help trapped souls for a living, and they're turned off by it. Truth is, my heart has always belonged to one man: Ford Pierce.

And he has no idea. He has only ever seen me as the little sister to his friend, Keaton. To him, I'm a nuisance that he has to chase out of Morton Manor and other similar places.

To Ford, I'm not a woman, I'm just Rylan, plain and simple.

I watch Mickey let herself into her house, then I pull away from the curb.

Out of habit, I scan the roadside as I drive home, searching for anything someone may have set out to be picked up. I nibble my thumbnail as I drive, my bracelet jangling as I work on a ragged area.

Then I see it, a small side table someone set out with the trash.

I try to drive by it, to ignore it.

I know I don't need it. I have too many tables as it is, but it calls to me. The table is useful and someone just threw it away.

As much as I know I don't need it, I know I'll take it home.

A mixture of excitement and guilt flutters in my chest as I pull over. I scan the street before I open my car door. Dark houses stretch in every direction. The side table sits near a streetlight, swims in a pool of brightness.

I slide out of the car and hurry to the table. It's an older one, the top veneer is cracked and one of the legs wobbles.

It's perfect. I tingle as I pick the table up and carry it to the backseat of my Caddy, thankful my mom left me a car that is so roomy.

With my treasure safe in the car, I drive to the house I also inherited from my mother. It's the house where I grew up and have lived most of my life, except for a few years when I had my own apartment.

I forgot to leave a light on when I went to do the show and the house is dark, a stark contrast to Mickey's. I park in the driveway because the garage is packed with treasures similar to the one on my backseat. Other precious finds I saved.

I carry the small table to the front door and let myself in. The mountain of boxes inside nearly blocks my entry. I step into the crowded room and take a deep breath. Inside, I feel safe. I set the table on top of a huge pile of items in the front room. "You're home now," I tell the table and myself.

I yawn so huge it makes my face hurt. I rub at the pain.

"Is that you, Rylan?" my mom's voice calls from her room at

the back of the house. I pick my way through the piles toward her.

"Just got back from taping." I don't tell her about the table I brought home. She never leaves her room anyway, has no idea about my collection that fills her house.

She waits for me, sitting on the side of her bed. "Did it go well?" she asks.

"It did." I leave out the details. What I do for a living is a sticky subject.

"Did you eat?" She always asks this.

"I grabbed a sandwich with Mickey on the way there," I lie from the doorway. I actually was too nervous to eat and now I'm too tired. My mom doesn't understand.

She reaches for her hairbrush and begins to run it through her hair. I have to look away. She has no idea that the back of her head has a huge hole in it. She has no idea she is actually dead.

Two years ago, my mother was shot to death in this very bed. I can still see her, but only here. At first, I tried to explain to her what happened. She stubbornly refused to believe me.

After a while, I gave up trying to make her see reality.

She brushes over the hole in her head, oblivious. I watch her in silence for a few minutes. Her hand freezes in mid-air, then drops the brush back on the red checked bedspread.

Mom turns her broken head. "Rylan are you home?" she asks.

Ghosts have short memories.

"Yes," I say sadly. "Good night, Mom."

"Did you eat?" she calls after me. I close her door and head to my room.

The hall is packed with stacks of books and clothes that I've dropped and left lying there. The floor feels squishy when I walk over the clothes to my room.

I don't look at the door to Keaton's room, buried behind a stack of books and boxes. I just pick my way through the hall.

My bed is covered in a mountain of blankets and throw pillows, the floor is full of stuffed animals I started collecting as a child. There's a large mix of other items in the room. I don't turn the light on, I just carefully follow the only empty path to my bed.

I lie down in my clothes and pull my favorite pink fuzzy blanket over my head. The sound machine is sitting on top of a pile of stuff, turned full volume to the sound of the sea.

I focus on the waves and seagulls, not on the whispers that seep in through the walls. The boxes and things block the sound somewhat, but the dead are restless and beg me to help. The hoard blocks them.

Frustrated with all the ghosts begging for my attention, I pull another blanket over my head. The fabric covers my face and makes me long for fresh air. I make a hole in the folds, just enough to breathe through. My bracelet jingles at the movement.

I finger the silver charms on it, each one meaningful. The largest of them is the silver cross Dad bought me for my sixteenth birthday. I run my finger over the familiar shape and pray for the voices to leave.

My whispered prayer is louder than the whispers of the ghosts begging to be let in. I repeat it until I fall asleep. "Lord, protect me and all that live in this home."

I know I'm alone, but I add Mom to the prayer just the same.

THREE

RYLAN FLYNN

I balance a travel coffee cup on the tiny edge of the kitchen counter that isn't crowded with stuff. Coffee is one of the few things I can make in my overly full kitchen.

Someday, I'll clean this mess.

Today is not that day.

Keaton and I are expected at Aunt Val's for our usual Friday morning ritual of French toast and family time. I look forward to my visits to Aunt Val's house in the woods. It is peaceful and secluded at Aunt Val's and blessedly free of ghosts.

Plus, she has a wonderful black lab mix, named George, whom I just adore. I always wanted a dog, but my house is barely livable for me, let alone if I brought a dog into the mix.

So I settle for visits with George.

When I pull into the small clearing at Aunt Val's, George is waiting on the front porch for me. He barks and bounces his greeting as I park near the A-frame home. He puts his paws up on my chest and I give him a big hug. His nails gently dig into my skin, but I don't mind.

"Sometimes I think you come just to see him," Aunt Val calls down from the porch.

I rub George behind the ears and smile. "He's a treat, but you know I come for the food," I tease. "Seriously, nothing better than something from your kitchen. Either here or down at the shop."

She gives an appreciative smile full of love. I come here for the smiles as much as the food.

"Well, hope you're hungry. I got some sausages at the farmer's market and they are to die for."

I gently push George off my chest and join Aunt Val on the wooden porch that runs the length of the front of her small house.

"Coffee?" she asks.

I hold up my travel mug, still half full. "I'm good for now." I sink into my usual rocking chair next to hers and groan in contentment. I scan the trees that are so close I would hit them if I threw a rock. The woods are lovely in the morning sun. Birds sing and a squirrel chatters.

George lies down next to my chair. I absent-mindedly rub his black head as I sip my coffee.

"This is just what I needed," I say, relaxed.

"Me too. The donut shop has been so busy this week. It's nice to have the morning off."

We sit in silence a few moments, until Val says, "Keaton called earlier and he's not coming today."

I look up in surprise. Ever since Mom died, our Friday breakfasts have been the one time I see my brother. "This is the third time this month he canceled," I complain.

Val shrugs. "He's a busy guy. Said he has a case he needs to work on this morning."

"He could work on it later," I grumble. I don't like the look of barely concealed hurt on my aunt's face. I, personally, don't want to deal with Keaton after my run-in with the police last night. He may not know about it yet, but Ashby's not that big and the town loves talking about me and what I do. Keaton's career at the District Attorney's office has really taken off the last year or so, and that means the fancy pants lawyer "has a reputation to protect." I don't want to hear the recriminations from my big brother, but I don't like that he hurt Aunt Val's feelings.

"Gotta make hay while the sun shines," Val says and rocks harder in her chair. George stands and climbs into the third, empty chair.

"There, we can pretend George is Keaton," I say to lighten the mood.

Val smiles over her coffee cup. "So, how's the show coming?"

I sit up straight, excited to talk about last night's encounter, and tell her about the ghost I talked to.

"You really saw her?" Val asks. "I thought the Morton Mistress was just a myth."

"Most myths have a grain of truth to them. She is definitely real."

I love that Val always believes me. When Mickey suggested a YouTube channel, Val was the one who convinced me to try it. Two years and thousands of followers later, I'm glad I agreed.

"Are you going to go back and talk to her again?"

"Ford warned me not to." I squirm in my seat a little.

Val looks at me knowingly. "Still hung up on that one, huh?"

My face burns. I hadn't realized she knew about my crush. "I'm not hung up on anyone."

"Uh-huh." She sips her coffee with a smug look, then changes the subject. "So, you hungry?"

My stomach chooses that moment to growl loudly. "I guess so." We both laugh.

Val bounces out of her chair and the screen door slaps shut

behind her. "Breakfast will be ready in a few. You keep George company."

I sit back in my chair, gently rocking. Closing my eyes, I listen to the woods surrounding us.

I feel someone watching me, that tickle on the back of my neck.

My eyes fly open and I check the driveway. I'm alone in the clearing.

I nervously finger my bracelet, counting the charms to fight the anxiety clawing in my belly.

The tingle is familiar; I thought I was safe from it here.

From the house, the smell of sausages cooking greets my nose. I focus on the smell, on the present. I don't want to see anything right now. I just want to enjoy the morning.

Inside the house, Val hums a tuneless song. Outside, the birds that sang so beautifully just moments ago are silent. Even the squirrel stopped chattering.

The clearing around Val's house seems to wait.

My mind sizzles, there's a spirit nearby.

I scan the trees again.

This time I see her. She hides behind a tree, dressed in a red T-shirt and jeans. She meets my eyes, then raises her hand, beckoning me to follow.

George growls low in his chest at the figure in the woods. "*Shh*," I soothe.

I leave my rocker, leave the porch, drawn to the young woman. Once she sees me coming, she turns and walks into the woods.

George whines and starts to follow me. I send him back to the porch and tell him to stay.

The young woman slips between the trees and I hurry to catch up to her.

"Rylan?" I hear Val calling, but I push through the trees and brush and follow the ghost.

My feet are loud on the dried leaves and I stumble over a fallen log in my haste, but I catch up to her.

"Where are you taking me?" I ask.

Her hair is pulled into a ponytail that swings as she turns her head. She cocks her head as if she's listening, then continues walking without answering.

I follow for several minutes through the woods. I'm not certain, but I think we are still on Aunt Val's property when she stops near a very large tree. I see ropes around the tree's wide trunk. The figure walks to the other side of the tree and I follow.

She's gone.

I look at the tree and gasp.

A body has been tied to it, wrapped tight in yellow ropes. It's the body of the girl I followed here. Her head hangs limply to the side. She looks like she's pretending to be dead, playing a part.

I touch her wrist to check for a pulse, but her skin is cold under my fingers.

Her dark ponytail has slid over her face, half hiding it from view. A hair has caught in her slightly parted lips. I want to move it for her, but I know better than to touch anything. As I watch, a fly climbs out of her mouth.

I step away from the tree and drop to my knees, a deep sorrow filling me. I talk to the dead that don't pass on, but besides finding Mom shot in the head in her bed, I've never seen a dead body. My stomach clenches and my mouth waters.

I lean over and retch up my morning coffee into the dried leaves. Some of it splatters onto my jeans.

"Rylan, what are you doing out here?" Val asks, walking around the tree with George. "Oh my," she says when she sees the girl. "What?"

George bounds around the tree, sniffs at my vomit, then sits and stares at the body. He lifts his muzzle and half-barks, half-howls into the silent woods.

Aunt Val fumbles in her pocket, digs out her phone. "Oh my, oh my," she repeats until they answer her call.

"This is Valerie Flynn. W-w-we just found a d-dead girl in my w-woods." She's so upset she begins to stutter like she did as a child.

FOUR

RYLAN FLYNN

I stare at the young woman's face as Aunt Val gives our location to the 911 operator. No more flies climb from her mouth, thankfully, but the image of her hanging against the ropes around the tree is disturbing. The dark ponytail blocks half of her features, but she looks to be a teenager, around seventeen or eighteen. She isn't wearing makeup, which surprises me.

Her feet are bare and turning black with pooled blood. Her hands are down at her sides, captured under the many rope loops binding her to the tree. Blood has pooled in them too, her fingers fat like black sausages.

Now that I look, I see the red T-shirt has a band logo on it. I recognize the name, Loose Gravel. The band often plays at The Lock Up, the bar down the street from my house. I've seen them play a few times. They must play somewhere else too, as this girl is too young to get into the bar.

Something glitters at the neck of the T-shirt. I lean closer. It's a necklace, broken and hanging over the collar of the shirt. A silver charm of a horse dangles from the end.

"How did you find her?" Aunt Val asks after hanging up the phone.

I scan the woods, looking for the ghost that led me here. "Her ghost told me to follow her."

Val pushes her lips together a moment and looks over her shoulder. "Is she still here?" she whispers.

"I don't see her. She just walked here and then disappeared."

"Can you get her back? We could ask her what happened." She keeps looking into the woods, turning her back on the body, petting George to keep him calm.

"It doesn't work like that. I wish it did. It would make my job easier. Often, they don't even realize they are dead."

"This one must if she led you here."

"She may not know why she is drawn to this place. She is probably more confused than we are."

"I don't understand how all this works. I mean, it's one thing to see a spirit at the Morton Mental Hospital, that place is creepy, but here in my woods? Why is she here? How did this happen so close to my house?" Val fires questions into the trees, not expecting an answer.

She suddenly turns.

"You don't think the police will think I had anything to do with this, will they?" She flicks her eyes at the body, but looks away quickly. "She's so close to my house. Seriously h-how d-did she get here?"

"Aunt Val, we need to stay calm. I'm sure the police will know you had nothing to do with this." I wave my arm in the direction of the road that Val told the dispatcher was close by. "Anyone could come into these woods."

She wipes the back of her hand across her mouth in agitation. "Right. I'm sure you're right. How are you so calm?"

"I'm not." I look at the splatter of vomited coffee and step away from it. Val looks at it, too.

"Oh. I feel nauseous, too." She places a hand on her belly.

"Oh, God. This poor girl." She tries to look at the body again, but can't.

I, on the other hand, can't look away. I study the girl's clothes, the rips in her jeans. My own jeans have rips in them, too, but I bought them that way. Her jeans are torn and sheared with a knife, deliberate.

I step closer and look at the skin behind. It is cut, but not deep. Dark smears of blood mar her pale skin.

"Hmm." I step back and check the other open places on the jeans. I find two more shallow cuts on her skin. Even her arms have a few cuts. Nothing serious, they wouldn't even need stitches. "How odd."

"What is it?" Val keeps her eyes on the ground.

"She has cuts on her. Several superficial cuts."

"Well, she was murdered."

"But they are shallow. None of them would cause her to bleed to death. I don't see where she was shot, and her neck doesn't have marks on it."

"Well, that's good, isn't it?"

"So how did she die?"

Val doesn't have an answer and neither do I.

We stand quietly, the birds once again calling and singing. Above us, a branch rubs on another making an eerie, lonesome sound.

Tears suddenly sting my eyes. The whole scene feels unreal and unbearably sad.

George nuzzles his nose against my hand and I kneel and throw my arms around his chest, thankful for the comfort.

Val sniffles, as caught up in the sadness as I am. "Such a waste."

I close my eyes and breathe in the dog scent of George's fur. In the distance toward the road, leaves crunch under heavy feet.

The police have arrived.

I lift my head and look through the trees. I see dark-blue

uniforms weaving our way. Two of the men are wearing polo shirts.

Ford Pierce and his partner Tyler Spencer.

My heart skips a beat and I wipe my eyes.

"They're here," Val says as I stand. George barks when he sees Ford and the other officers.

Val takes his collar and tells him to hush.

Ford is the first one to reach the tree.

"Rylan, I didn't expect to see you here."

"Rylan's the one that found her," Val says. I didn't want him to know that. The next question is inevitable.

"How did you know she was out here?" he asks, looking at the girl on the tree.

"This is out in the middle of nowhere," Tyler adds.

"I. Um, actually George found her," I lie. "He ran into the woods and I followed him here."

Ford looks over his shoulder, away from the body. I can tell he doesn't believe me. "The dog?"

"Yep." I want to tell the truth, but I know Ford and Tyler and the other officers joining us will not understand that the spirit of the dead girl led me here.

He shrugs and lets it go. Val puts her hand on my shoulder. "Maybe we should go back to the house and let these officers do their job."

"Good idea," Tyler says. "We'll come get your statements when we're done here."

Ford is looking around the scene, sees my vomit and looks at me with concern in his blue eyes.

"Yeah, that's mine," I say, my face burning hot. He didn't even flinch when he saw the body but I lost my coffee. "Sorry about that."

"Understandable," Ford says, then turns back to work.

"Marrero is here," Tyler says.

A man with a white, flat-top haircut is walking toward us,

trudging heavily through the woods. His jacket says "coroner" on the chest. He has a team of three following him. He ducks under the crime-scene tape another officer is stringing between trees to join us.

The coroner barely glances at the girl tied to the tree and focuses on George. "Get this dog out of my crime scene, please," he says to Val, who is holding his collar.

"Right, sorry," Val says, backing away from the imposing man.

"Dr. Henry Marrero, this is Valerie Flynn. The dog found the body."

Val holds out her hand for a handshake, but Marrero busies himself with slipping on a plastic glove and ignores her.

"I'm Rylan," I say, stepping between Val and the rude coroner. He flicks his eyes in my direction, but doesn't respond. Instead, he starts giving directions to his team.

Ford looks at me apologetically. "We'll come get your statements soon." He turns back to the body. We've been dismissed.

The crime tape encircles the site now and we have to duck under it to leave. George bounds ahead as we crunch our way back to the house, each of us lost in thought.

"Coffee?" Val asks as we climb the steps to her porch.

"Definitely." I retrieve my empty travel cup from where I left it and follow her inside.

"That Marrero is a peach," Val says sarcastically as I sit at the kitchen bar. "He comes into the shop sometimes, but only orders coffee. Black. Never sugar or cream. I guess he doesn't recognize me."

"He doesn't seem like the type to remember faces. At least not of the living." I try for a joke, but it falls flat.

We're both thinking of the dead girl, so close to Val's house.

"I didn't hear a thing last night," Val muses. "How could this happen so nearby?"

I stand and look out the kitchen window in the direction of

the crime scene. "I wish she would come back and talk to me, then we could find out. I doubt Ford will tell us much."

A shadow moves in the trees and I press my face close to the glass. Was that the ghost? I don't have the tingling I often get when a spirit is near.

Val joins me at the window. "Do you see her?"

"I don't think so. It was just a shadow from a branch moving."

We stand together watching the trees, wondering what they are finding out about the girl. I sip coffee and it makes my stomach lurch. Such violence shouldn't be this close to Val's house. Shouldn't even be in Ashby. I quietly take Val's hand in mine and we stand together, watching the woods.

"Do you think she will come back?" I ask after several silent minutes.

"You know much better than me." Val turns away from the window. "I don't suppose you want breakfast?"

"Not really, sorry."

"Me either."

She takes the French toast and sausage she made and feeds it to George. He scarfs it down eagerly, happy for the treat.

Val washes the dishes as I continue to stare out the window. After what seems like a very long time, a cruiser parks next to my old Cadillac. Ford and Tyler Spencer climb out.

"They're here," I say, and run a hand over my hair.

I watch as they scan the property while they climb the steps to the porch. Val opens the door before they can knock.

"Mrs. Flynn," Tyler says.

"Ms. not Mrs.," Val corrects him quietly.

"Of course. Ms. Flynn," Tyler says.

"Come in," she says, stepping away from the door.

George growls low in his chest and Val quiets him. "Sorry. I don't get many visitors. Except for Rylan and her brother."

"I saw Keaton this morning," Ford says, lightening the

mood. "He was at The Hole getting coffee and so was I." I make a mental note that I need to stop by Val's donut shop, The Hole, more often if Ford is in there regularly.

"So." Tyler takes the lead of the conversation. "How exactly did the dog find the body this morning?"

I can tell by his barely hidden sarcasm that he doesn't believe our story. This isn't going to be a statement; it's an interrogation.

FIVE

RYLAN FLYNN

"Just as we told you," I say. Ford focuses his eyes on my face and I feel heat crawl into my cheeks. "Coffee?" I turn away from his intensity and refill my cup.

"We're good," Ford says. I feel his gaze on my back. "You know, Rylan, it's a long way from here to that tree. I don't see why this dog—"

"—George. His name is George," I interrupt as I turn back to the group.

"Right. I don't see why George would be out there."

I pretend casualness. "You don't know George."

Ford's eyes narrow and I can tell he doesn't believe me. I fiddle with my charm bracelet, the jangle loud in the waiting silence.

"Is that how you want to play it?"

Tyler looks from me to Ford, confusion coloring his features.

"Yep." I stare him down.

"Okay, so George ran into the woods and you followed him and found the woman?"

"That's right," Val offers, backing me up.

"Do you know who she is?" I ask.

"There was no ID on her, so not yet," Tyler says.

"That poor girl," Val murmurs. "Any idea how she died or how she got into my woods?"

Ford and Tyler exchange a look. "We hoped you could tell us," Tyler says.

"Me?" Val's surprise is genuine. "I don't know anything about it."

"She is on your property," Tyler says.

"So? I don't know how she got there."

Tyler looks thoughtful for a moment, then drops the line I feared. "Where were you last night between 10p.m. and 2 a.m.?"

"Now wait, you can't be serious." I look to Ford for help. He won't meet my eyes.

"I was here," Val explains.

"Alone? Can anyone verify that?" Tyler pushes.

"I was with George." Val looks at the dog. "I don't suppose that counts." She also looks at Ford for help. "You two don't think I did that to that poor girl." Her voice rises in agitation.

Ford looks at Val. "Do you know her?"

Val swallows hard and looks at the floor. "I've seen her at the donut shop, but I don't 'know' her. I don't know her name or anything. Just that she likes the lemon-jelly filled."

All three of us stare at Val. "You didn't say anything out in the woods," I say.

Val shrugs and fiddles with her short hair. "I wasn't sure at first. But now that I had some time to get over the shock, she did look familiar."

Tyler takes his phone out of his pocket and pulls up a picture. "Look at her face." He holds his phone for her, a photo of the young woman on the screen. "You sure you don't know her name?"

Val flicks her eyes at the screen and then away. "I'm sorry. Truly, I am. I never knew her name."

"Credit card receipts?" Ford asks. "Would there be one of those?"

Val shakes her head. "I don't think so. I'm not sure, but I think she always paid with cash." Val chews on her bottom lip, thinking. "Wait. Kimmie. I feel like she knows Kimmie Steele that works for me."

Ford jots the name down in his book. "Do you know where we can find this Kimmie?"

Val looks at the clock to check the time. "She works Friday mornings as part of her school program. She should be at the shop now."

Ford flips his book closed with a snap. "Thank you for your time," he says politely to Val, shaking her hand.

Tyler shakes it, too. "We may be back for more questions. In the meantime, don't leave town and all that."

Val swallows, then asks, "Am I a suspect?"

"Everyone is a suspect until this is solved." Tyler looks at me pointedly. "We already know where you were last night."

I put my shoulders back. "Working."

Tyler shakes his head a little and heads for the door.

Ford has the grace to look sheepish. "We'll be in touch," he says and opens the door to leave. He lets Tyler onto the porch first, then leans so close I can smell him. I want to breathe deeply, but resist the urge.

"You know you can tell me the truth about how you found her," he says, so low that Tyler won't hear. "I know there's more to your story. If you have any information that would be helpful to the investigation, you need to tell me."

I widen my eyes and try to look innocent. "I don't know anything."

Ford looks disappointed that I'm continuing my lie. He

seems to want to say more, but suddenly turns and walks away without another word.

"You should have told him the truth," Val says, looking over my shoulder.

"That wouldn't serve me too well. I don't want to be involved in this."

A shadow moves in the woods and I glimpse a flash of red T-shirt, with the yellow Loose Gravel logo. George growls low in his chest.

Val follows my gaze. "Is she out there again?"

I tear my eyes away from the figure. "Behind that tree, across the clearing."

The cruiser is backing up and I feel Ford's eyes on me. He looks from me to where I am staring at the girl, a question on his face. Of course, he can't see her, but he looks irritated. He shakes his head and moves off down the driveway, disappearing into the trees.

Val and I wait on the porch to be sure the car is gone. The figure peeks around the tree again, searching for me.

"I'm going to try to talk to her."

"Do you want me to come?" Val sounds scared.

I squeeze her hand in reassurance. "No. That might frighten her off. She's probably confused and terrified." I start down the porch steps. "Stay here."

George growls again. Val puts him in the house and shuts the door.

The figure steps from behind the tree when she sees me crossing the clearing.

"Don't be scared," I tell her, holding my hands wide. "I just want to talk."

She waits.

I approach slowly. "Do you know where you are?" I ask.

Her face scrunches in confusion and she shakes her head.

"You are at my aunt's house. Do you know how you got here?"

She makes a gurgling sound in her throat that seems to startle her. Then she shakes her head again, so hard her ponytail flips.

"What's your name?" I ask, hoping to help the investigation.

She repeats the gurgling sound. Her eyes grow wide with fear and she puts her hands to her neck.

"Can you talk?" I ask gently.

More gurgling. She begins to panic and claw at her throat.

"Stay calm." I realize how she died. When they come to me, they are exactly like they were at the moment of death. This poor girl must have choked on something that is still in her throat. "I think you have something stuck in your throat." I step closer. "Can you open your mouth?"

She tips her head back and I look inside. Just as I feared, way in the back, I see something shiny.

"You choked on something."

Her nostrils flare as she breathes deep, her face full of terror.

"Don't be scared. I know this is all new. Do you remember what happened?"

The ponytail flies again as she shakes her head. Her eyes plead with me for help.

"I can't take it out. I'm sorry to be the one to tell you, but you were murdered last night."

Her eyes widen so far, I can see the whites all around the brown centers.

She shakes her head again, hard and fast, her eyes begging for it not to be true.

"I know this is hard to take in," I say as gently as I can. "I can help you."

She stops shaking her head and listens. "You need to cross over. There is nothing for you here now."

She backs away from me, moving silently over the crunchy leaves.

"Don't leave. I want to help you," I plead.

The girl turns and flees into the woods. A moment later, she disappears.

I watch the place where she vanished, hoping she'll come back. The woods remain empty.

I turn back to my aunt waiting on the porch, her face full of worry.

As I cross the clearing, the birds begin singing again. Their lively sound feels wrong after talking to a dead girl.

"What did she say? Did she tell you what happened?"

I shake my head. "No. She can't talk. There's something metal in her throat."

"That's awful. Is that what killed her?"

"I guess so. It would explain why there are no marks on her besides those shallow cuts."

Val looks into the woods. "I'm not going to sleep tonight knowing she's out there."

"She's harmless. She's just scared."

"Well, she scares me just the same."

I'm suddenly tired and hungry. Seeing spirits often drains me, and I haven't eaten since yesterday afternoon.

"I know we didn't eat the French toast this morning," I start.

"I'll make you some more," she says quickly. "I need something to do to keep me busy. I don't like all the police lurking around. And that poor girl." With a shake of her head and a last look into the trees, Val returns to the house. Her shoulders are slumped, and I fear this might all be too much for her.

SIX

FORD PIERCE

The look on Rylan's face as we pull out grabs my interest. She's focused on something in the trees, but I don't see anything when I look.

Is she seeing something beyond this realm? The same thing I suspect she saw this morning, which led her to the dead woman in the woods?

I wish she'd tell me the truth. The investigation relies on facts, not made-up stories. I'm hoping we'll get some from Kimmie Steele at The Hole.

The sweet smell of donuts and coffee fills the brick-walled restaurant. The beaten wooden floor and large windows overlooking the courthouse square are lovely. I know cops and donuts is a cliché, but The Hole is a favorite stop for everyone in Ashby.

Eileen behind the counter smiles when we enter.

"More coffee, detectives?" she asks with a smile.

"No, thank you. We're actually here to speak to Kimmie Steele. Is she working?"

Eileen loses the smile and grows concerned. "She got here a few hours ago. She works mornings after she checks in at school.

A good girl. She's in the back right now." She looks over her shoulder toward the back room. "Is everything okay?"

"Can we speak to her, please?" Tyler asks.

I hate what we are about to do. If this Kimmie knows the girl in the woods, we will change her life forever.

Eileen wants to say more, but disappears through the swinging double doors behind the counter. A few moments later a fresh-faced blond emerges.

"Kimmie Steele?" I ask.

"Yes," she says hesitantly, wiping her hands on her green apron.

I ask Eileen, "Is there somewhere we can talk in private?"

"Of course. The office is right through that door and to the left. You detectives just take as long as you need. Don't worry, Kimmie, I'm sure it will all be all right."

Once we are secluded in the office and Kimmie is sitting down, I begin the task of questioning her.

"You're starting to scare me," Kimmie says. "Is my family okay?"

"Yes," I tell her. "This isn't about your family." I wish I didn't have to do this, but it must be done. "This is about a young woman that was found deceased this morning. We believe you might know her."

Kimmie's hand flies to her mouth. "Oh no. Who is it?"

"That's what we are hoping you can tell us," Tyler says, taking out his phone and pulling up the picture he showed Val. "This is a bit gruesome, but we really need to find out who she is."

Kimmie looks at the phone. Her sharp intake of breath tells me she recognizes the girl. Tears instantly spring to her eyes and she looks away.

"It's Celeste."

I flip open my notebook. "Celeste?"

She nods and wipes at her nose with the back of her hand. I find a napkin on the desk and hand it to her.

"That's Celeste Monroe. She just moved here a few weeks ago from Toledo. I don't know her real well, but we've hung out a few times."

"Do you go to school with her?"

"No. She graduated last year back home." Kimmie wipes her nose. "What happened? How did she die?"

I can't make eye contact. "She was murdered."

Another sharp intake of breath and Kimmie sniffles. "Poor Celeste. Who did it?"

"We don't know, yet," Tyler says. "What else can you tell us about her?"

"I don't know much. She dates a guy in the band that plays around here, Loose Gravel. From what she told me, that's why she moved to Ashby, to be with him."

I recognize the band name from Celeste's T-shirt.

"Do you know this guy's name?" I ask.

Kimmie shakes her head. "I've seen them play, but I don't know them real well. Drew maybe?"

"Do you know her family?"

"No. I got the feeling she wasn't really close to them."

"Do you know any of her other friends?"

Kimmie thinks a moment before answering. "Like I said, we hung out a few times, but I don't know her well. I've seen her with Marie Prestwood a bit. I'm sure she'll know more." She dabs at her eyes with the napkin. "You will catch this guy, right?"

"We will do our best," I hedge. I learned long ago not to promise anything to anyone.

Tyler fishes out a business card. "If you think of anything else that might help us, even a tiny detail, give me a call."

Kimmie takes the card and stares at it, as if the answer to Celeste's murder is printed there. "I will."

We leave Kimmie and say goodbye to Eileen. Out on the sidewalk, the sun is so bright it hurts my eyes.

"Where to next?" Tyler asks.

"Next we need to track down her family in Toledo and tell them what happened."

The thought of telling a family they've lost a daughter makes me sick to my stomach, but as lead on the case, it is my responsibility.

"You find them and make the call and then let's track down Marie Prestwood. She should be in school right now," Tyler says as we climb back into our cruiser and turn toward the station.

Telling Celeste's mother about what happened adds another scar to my heart. Listening to a mother cry is never easy. I give her the few details we know and tell her how sorry I am for her loss. After I promise I'll talk to her tomorrow, I hang up gratefully.

I run a hand over my face and Tyler looks at me with concern from his desk next to mine.

"Bad?" he asks.

"Always is," I say with a heavy sigh. "Let's get out there and catch this guy. Did you find out where Marie Prestwood is?"

"Like we figured, she is in class at the high school." Tyler grabs the keys off his desk and heads for the door. I follow with a heavy heart.

Principal Baxter at Ashby High School seems concerned to see us. "I will send someone to bring Marie here," she says, sinking into her seat behind her desk. "Such a sad day."

"Yes, ma'am," Tyler says into the awkward silence. Principal Baxter plays with her pen, stacks some papers.

"This girl was murdered?" she finally asks. "Are you sure?"

"We're sure," I say, straightening the crease in my slacks. After several tense minutes, there is a soft knock on the door.

"Principal Baxter?" A teenage girl opens the door and hesitates in the hall.

"Marie, come in," Baxter says, waving the girl inside.

Marie's eyes dart to the badge on my belt, then settle on the gun at my hip. "What's going on?"

The principal invites Marie to take the empty seat next to her. She sits down on the very edge of the chair, her eyes wide.

I flip open my notebook and lean forward, making my face look as comforting as possible. The girl looks terrified. "Marie, do you know Celeste Monroe?"

She squirms in her seat. "Yes. Why?"

"I'm sorry to have to tell you, but she is deceased." I brace for the inevitable emotional response.

Marie just blinks. "Celeste? Dead? How?"

"She was murdered last night. We understand you were friends with her."

She nods and begins gnawing on a thumbnail, staring at the wall behind me, unable to meet my eyes.

"When's the last time you saw her?"

"Last night, around eight. We were hanging out at my house, listening to music."

I write that down. "How did she seem? Did she seem nervous about anything or tell you about any problems?"

She chews on her thumbnail, thinking. "She was a bit on edge. She'd talked to her mom earlier and I figured she was just shook up about that."

"How did you two meet?" Tyler chimes in.

Marie sits taller. "She is dating the drummer for the band Loose Gravel. I follow the band. They were playing at The Lock Up and we ended up dancing next to each other. We just kind of hit it off after that."

"The Lock Up is not an underage club," Tyler points out.

Marie squirms in her seat. "I have a fake ID. You won't tell my dad, will you?"

"We're not interested in your ID right now," I tell her. "Do you know the name of the drummer she is dating?"

"Drew something or other. He buys us drinks sometimes. He seems okay."

"Do you know where Drew lives?" Tyler asks.

"No. But they are playing at The Lock Up again tonight. I'm sure you can find him there."

"Did Celeste and Drew get along? Did you see any concerns there?"

"Drew's cool. He seems devoted to Celeste, when he's not playing in the band, and keeps his eyes on her. She moved here from Toledo to be with him. They met when he played a show there and that was that."

"Do they live together?" I'm surprised that if they are so close, Drew hasn't contacted us looking for her.

"No. He lives with the band. She thought they were going to live together but now she rents a small apartment. I don't know how she affords it. She doesn't have a job yet, but she's only been here a few weeks."

"Do you have any ideas on who might have hurt Celeste?" I ask.

A shadow seems to cross Marie's features, then it disappears. "No," she says simply.

She looks away from the wall and starts staring at my shoes. "Are you sure? Anything you can think of might help the investigation."

Marie shakes her head. "I can't think of anything or anyone."

We wrap up the conversation and leave the school, but I can't shake the feeling that Marie knows more than she's telling.

SEVEN

RYLAN FLYNN

With my belly full of Aunt Val's French toast, I return home a while later. I don't know what to do about the girl in the woods or her spirit that is wandering there. I want to call Ford and ask about the investigation, but I know he won't tell me anything. I wonder if they figured out who the girl is.

What I want more than anything is my mom. I let myself into the house and take a deep breath as my possessions swallow me in their embrace. The house smells like dust mixed with the remnants of Mom's perfume.

It smells like home.

"Is that you, Rylan?" Mom calls from her room.

"I'm home," I call, heading down the path between boxes and furniture to her bedroom door. "Before you ask, Aunt Val already fed me."

Mom is looking out the window of her room, a pensive tightness in her face. "Did that bush always have flowers on it?" she asks, pointing into the backyard. Usually, Mom isn't aware of the passage of time, she's lost in her own form of reality. When she catches glimpses of the here and now, she gets confused.

"It always has flowers on it," I lie. It's easier to lie than to tell her she's dead and answer all her questions, like I used to. She leans close to the glass, studies the bush. "Maybe you're right." She turns with a flourish of her nightgown. "Now, how's my girl?"

"Not great." I sit on her bed and run a finger along the red checked pattern.

She sits next to me on the bed. "What happened?"

I want to tell her everything, but I'm not sure I should. I give into the temptation and tell her about the ghost of the woman and following her to the tree. "There was a young woman tied there. She was dead."

Mom pats my hand and my skin goes cold from the touch. "You poor thing. That must have been terrifying."

I look at her pale face, her blood-matted hair. I stare at the hole behind her ear that is more terrifying than anything I saw this morning.

I pull my eyes away. "It was."

"What did the police say?"

"Ford and his partner, Tyler Spencer, asked us some questions and even hinted that maybe Aunt Val had something to do with it."

Mom jumps to her feet. "That's nonsense. Brett's sister would never do such a horrible thing. She is the sweetest, kindest... Oh, that makes me mad."

"I think Ford and Tyler know that. But they had to ask."

Mom rubs her hands together in agitation. "Shameful. They need to be looking for the real killer."

"I know, Mom. And they are. They just have to be thorough."

"What are you going to do?"

"What am *I* going to do? What do you mean?"

"The ghost of this girl came to you for help. You can't turn your back on her now."

"What can I do? I'm not a detective."

"You're a paranormal investigator. So investigate."

"What I do is not the same as tracking a killer."

"Then do it your way. Talk to the ghost and find out what happened."

"I tried that. There is something in her throat, the thing that killed her. She can't talk. I don't even know if she realizes she's dead." I wish I hadn't said that last part, it hits a little too close to home with Mom's situation.

"I'm sure she realizes it. How could she not?"

I quickly move on. "I don't think Ford would like me poking around his case."

"Then too bad for Ford."

I bristle a little in defense. "He's just doing his job."

Mom softens. "I know. I just don't like him going after Val."

"He's moved on now." I chew on my lower lip a moment, thinking. Mom returns to the window and looks out. "I suppose I could try to talk to the girl again," I say. "Maybe I'll find something useful."

"Go to your dad. You two help the ghosts together. I'm sure he can assist in this."

Dad. I hadn't thought of including him in this.

Mom leans close to the glass and asks, "Has that bush always had flowers on it?" My heart grows heavy. I like to pretend Mom is still here, still alive. Times like this, it's painfully clear she's not.

"It's always had flowers on it," I say and stand from the bed. I wish I could hug her, but I leave the room instead.

Mom is right, I need to talk to Dad about this.

I know where to find him on a Friday. He'll be in his office at the Pine Grove Chapel where he serves as head pastor. It only takes a few minutes to drive through Ashby's tree-lined side streets to his church, tucked away near the center of town.

The white chapel with deep, red front steps is snuggled below two large oak trees.

Dad has helped me deal with ghosts before. As a pastor, he is very aware of the forces of good and evil in the world. As a man, he truly cares what happens to people and their souls. He sees my work as a last chance to redeem.

I climb the steps to the front door of the historic chapel, keeping my head down. There is a small cemetery between the church and the large Victorian home next to it, and sometimes the departed make themselves known.

I feel the tingle on the back of my neck that means someone is watching me. The tingle is strong and I know it is a spirit. I hesitate at the doorway, I have enough on my plate today, I don't need another ghost in my life. Almost against my will, I turn around.

The little girl stands at the bottom of the steps, dressed in a long white nightgown, her long hair mussed. I've seen her many times, but usually in the distance. She's never approached me before. I've seen her tombstone and know that she died at the tender age of six.

Up close, the illness that darkens under her eyes is in stark contrast to the paleness of her skin.

"Hello?" I say gently. She steps back, nervous. "Can I help you in some way?"

She looks across the yard to the cemetery. "Have you seen Mommy?"

"I'm sorry, darling. I have not seen her."

The door behind me rattles and opens. "Rylan? I was just stepping out for lunch," my dad says.

The girl looks startled, then disappears.

Dad seems confused. "Were you talking with someone?"

"Sarah was here." Dad is familiar with the little ghost. I've told him about her and we both wish we could help her cross over. She's so skittish around me, this is the first time she's ever spoken.

Dad looks across the yard to the cemetery. "Is she still here?" he asks, full of hope.

"Not now. But she asked me if I've seen her mommy."

He stares across the grass, his face pinched in concern. "She's been dead for over a century. I hate to think of her roaming around here alone all that time." He shakes his head a little, then brightens. "To what do I owe this surprise visit?" He puts an arm around my shoulder and gives me a squeeze.

"I need your help with something. Can we go in and talk for a bit?"

His face grows pinched again. "Are you okay?" He opens the front door for me.

"Yeah, I'm okay, it's nothing like that." I follow him into the cool, dim building. A feeling of peace washes over me. I close my eyes a moment and say a quick prayer, "Thank you, Lord, for all my blessings," I murmur.

Dad is smiling when I open my eyes, but doesn't comment.

"Let's go into my office." He leads me down a short hall to the small office that my mom decorated for him nearly twenty years ago. He hasn't changed a thing, even after they divorced.

I sit down in a cracked leather chair. He takes the one beside me instead of the one behind his desk, with the placard reading Pastor Brett Flynn. "Now, what's going on?"

I tell him about the ghost in the woods and how I found her dead. Dad is used to my stories of ghosts, has helped me several times. This time I surprise him.

"You found a dead body? A murdered girl?" he asks in awe. "Were you scared?"

I think of my puking on the leaves. "Yes. I won't lie. I was pretty freaked. I'm used to the dead, but I don't normally see their bodies."

He looks down at his desk, fiddles with his pen. I can tell he's thinking of when I found Mom.

"That was different," I venture.

He gives a little shake of his head. "Right. It was. So how can I help with this?"

"I'm not sure. I just feel like I'm supposed to do something for this young woman. I tried talking to her, but she can't speak. I think she choked to death on something metal."

"Did you tell Ford and his partner this?"

"No. I don't want to explain how I know it. Besides, the coroner will figure it out and know for sure."

"Did you meet Coroner Marrero?"

"He's definitely something," I say sarcastically.

"Yeah. I've dealt with him a few times. He is definitely set in his ways. That job must make you hard-hearted."

"Marrero isn't my problem. Hopefully, this is my last crime scene."

"Hopefully," Dad agrees. "So how do you want to proceed? Do you want to help her cross over?"

"I feel like this one is a bit bigger than that. She came to me. I feel like I need to help figure out what happened to her. How did she get into Val's woods? Who killed her?"

Dad sits forward in his chair. "You cannot go chasing after a killer. That is a job for Ford and the rest of the police."

"But she came to me."

"To find her. Without you, she'd still be tied to that tree. I'd hate to think how long she'd be out there."

I gnaw on my shredded thumbnail for a few moments. I know he's right. I should leave it alone. I just can't.

"Will you help me talk to her? I want to go tonight and try to contact her again. I'll invite Mickey too. If I get any information, it will be good to have it on tape to show Ford."

Dad studies my face. "You're going to pump a ghost that can't talk for information?"

I shrug one shoulder. "There are other ways to communicate. She can nod."

He stands, excited. "Okay. I'm in."

"The moon is still full, too, so we have that on our side."

Dad smiles indulgently. "You really think this will work?"

"I've investigated ghosts before, this is just like that."

"Except most of the time, they aren't murder victims. What if the killer finds out you are poking around?"

"How would he know?" I honestly hadn't thought of that, but I won't back down now. "And you'll be with me. Mickey too."

"Okay." He spreads his hands in acceptance.

"Let's meet at Val's." I stand and kiss his cheek. "Be prepared to help her cross over once we are done. The poor thing has been through enough already, she deserves peace."

"I will." He pulls me close and I sink into his strong arms, enjoying the hug I couldn't get from Mom. "Your brother is going to have a fit when he finds out."

"Then don't tell him," I reply breezily. "See you tonight." I escape down the hall.

As I pass by the main church sanctuary, I make a quick detour to the altar. I kneel at the rail and bow my head. "Please help me to help this young woman," I say in a low voice. "Amen."

I leave the sanctuary and walk out into the bright sunlight, scanning the area for Sarah's ghost. I catch a quick flash that might be her white nightgown, ducking behind a stone statue of an angel. After a few steps in her direction, my phone rings.

I check the screen. It's my brother, Keaton.

"Holy flip, he must know."

I take a deep breath and hit answer.

EIGHT

RYLAN FLYNN

I press the phone to my ear, bracing for Keaton's greeting. "Hey," I say nervously, crossing the parking area.

"I hear you've been busy," he says without preamble.

I try for nonchalance as I climb into my car. "Oh, yeah? How's that?" I scan the cemetery for the little girl, but she has disappeared.

"Don't be coy with me, Rylan. I heard about you finding that girl this morning. The whole office is buzzing with it."

"I can't help what your co-workers talk about," I say, my defenses rising as they often do when talking to my brother.

He blows out air in exasperation. "How did you find that girl way out in the woods? Or do I need to ask?"

For a lawyer stuck securely in reality, my life's work is a never-ending source of frustration to Keaton. Publicly, he barely accepts it. Privately, he believes in my abilities.

"The girl's ghost led me to her." I tell him the truth. I've learned that trying to dupe him never leads to anything good.

"I figured as much." He sounds disappointed.

"Sorry that me getting caught up in a murder investigation is cramping your style," I retort.

"It's not that." He blows out air again. "You know I just worry about you."

"Yeah, you worry. But it's about your reputation, not about me."

"That's not fair."

"Neither is this phone call. I didn't ask the ghost of that girl to come find me. She just did."

"What about last night? Did that ghost ask you to break into the old hospital and trespass?"

I should be surprised that he knows I was tossed out of the asylum by the police last night, but I'm not. From his office at the District Attorney's law office, somehow, he hears about everything in this town.

"That was different. That was work."

"You need a different line of work."

"My thousands of fans would disagree," I retort, putting the car in reverse. I've heard his complaints enough times in the past, I'm not in the mood now. I understand that being assistant to the District Attorney has some strings tied to it, but I won't change who I am for his job.

"Seriously, are you okay?" he asks in a rare tender moment. "You've not seen many dead bodies. At least, not in real life."

I've seen more dead than he will ever understand, each of them in the state they died in. But I take his point as caring.

"I'm okay. Aunt Val was with me. She was pretty shook up, too."

There is a heavy silence on the line. "Val didn't need that," he finally says.

I grip the steering wheel tighter. "I didn't plan for her to be there."

"Right, I know," he backpedals.

"Listen, I've got to go to work. Mickey and I are editing last night's footage today.

He lowers his voice into a whisper. "Did you really see her? You talked to the Morton Mistress?"

"I did," I state boldly.

"Cool," he says, then seems to catch himself. "Of course, you shouldn't be trespassing."

I take the compliment and let the rest slide. It's more than I usually get from Keaton.

"Call Val and check on her, will you? I'm sure she'd want to hear from you after you missed our breakfast this morning." I can't stop myself from adding the slight, but I instantly regret it.

His voice grows tight. "I will." Then he hangs up without saying goodbye.

I drive through town, toward Mickey's, mulling over my conversation, mentally kicking myself for the last part. Keaton tries, he really does.

I almost believe it.

Mickey's new husband, Marco, is mowing the lawn when I park in front of their house. He waves and smiles as I make my way up the walk. After my conversation with Keaton, I appreciate the friendly gesture.

I let myself in through Mickey's front door, calling, "I'm here."

Mickey's house is the opposite of mine. Everything is neat and organized, the floors are clear and there aren't piles of boxes and found furniture everywhere. It's so neat it kind of gives me the creeps.

I'm sure Mickey would say my house creeps her out, if I ever let her inside. We always work on the show here. My collections are my business.

"I'm in the office," Mickey says and I follow her voice down the hall. She lets out a string of colorful expletives.

I grow cold when I see her pinched face. "What's wrong?"

"It's all gone, all of it."

My stomach sinks. "Not last night's footage?"

She turns a tortured face to me. "Yes. It was here after we finished with the shoot, but now it's gone." She turns the camera over and gives it a little shake as if that will make the video appear.

"It can't be." I take my seat next to her at the desk and look at the camera, and then at the computer screen. Mickey handles all the technical stuff. I have no idea what I'm looking at.

Tears of frustration make her eyes gleam. "I'm so sorry. I know what talking to her meant."

I take a breath and pat her hand. "This sucks, but it's not your fault."

"I just don't understand. I checked it last night after I got home. It was there. Now nothing."

I sit back in my chair, my mind already spinning with a solution. "Don't worry. We'll go talk to the Morton Mistress again another time."

"You're awful calm. We don't have anything for this week's episode."

"We'll get something tonight. Did you hear about what I found this morning?"

Mickey lifts her bangs then lets them fall. "I have been home all day. What happened?"

I tell her about the ghost leading me to her body and trying to talk to me after.

"A murder victim came to find you? That's one of the coolest things you've done."

"I don't know about cool, but it was an eventful morning. Tonight should be eventful, too."

Mickey sits on the edge of her office chair. "Are we going to talk to her?"

I love that my best friend is always up for an adventure. It comes in handy in our line of work.

"We are. Dad is coming, too. I'm hoping we can get some information that will assist the investigation. Then we can help her cross over."

She looks at the camera, her face once again tense. "Hopefully, we'll get some good video."

"I'm sure we will. Now stop worrying about the missing footage." I catch a shadow moving in the hall. It flits away before I can get a good look. I've seen this shadow before, always out of the corner of my eye. Whoever or whatever it is doesn't want me to see them. I get the feeling it is a young boy, full of mischief.

I'd bet anything the boy is responsible for the missing footage.

Mickey follows my gaze out into the hall. "Did you see him this time?"

"No, he was watching, though. Probably getting a kick out of the mess he put us in."

Mickey shakes herself. "I don't know how you do it, seeing them everywhere you go. Freaks me out just knowing there's a ghost here, even if I've never seen him."

I shrug. She's said these words before. Mickey's been my friend since middle school. She was the first one I told about seeing spirits. She believes me completely, but it must be odd for her not to see them.

"Never seen who?" Marco ducks his head into the office. I hadn't realized the mower stopped outside.

Mickey gives me a startled look. Marco doesn't know about the spirit who lives in their house, and Mickey would like to keep it that way.

"We're just talking about a case," I say, standing.

Marco accepts it with ease. "I'm about out of gas in the mower. Gonna run up to the gas station. Do you need anything?"

"No, I'm good." She stands and plants a quick kiss on his

cheek. I look away. "We've got to work tonight." Mickey looks to me for the details.

"We are meeting Dad at Aunt Val's."

"Does this have to do with the body you found?" Marco asks.

"How do you know about that?" asks Mickey.

"Mr. Howard just told me. He said the story is all over town that there was a dead girl found in the woods this morning." He nods. "Your name might have been mentioned."

"Great," I say sarcastically. "Just what I need. More rumors about me."

"Not a rumor if it's true," Marco says, teasing. "That's called news."

Mickey slaps him playfully on the arm. "Leave her be. She's had a rough enough day. And yes, tonight we are going to try to talk to the girl."

Marco jingles his keys. "You ladies have fun hunting ghosts. I've got a lawn to mow." With that, he heads back outside.

"He's horrible," Mickey says, her voice full of love.

I'd take that kind of horrible any day.

NINE

It went wrong.

It went wrong.

She was perfect, but it went wrong.

The cuts were the best part. Long slices and thin lines of blood.

"More blood," the voice says from the painting of my mother. "This time more blood."

I stare at her unmoving face captured in oil long ago. "Whatever you need." I hate the supplication in my voice but cannot stop it. "Whatever it takes."

"Try again. This time use the other coin," the painting says.

"I will." I raise a shaking finger to the painting, touch the brush strokes tenderly.

"And more blood. You should know better."

I look away from her face. "Yes."

Again, I get to do it again.

My own blood sings at the thought. I leave the talking painting and enter the room down the hall. I used to be allowed in this room only under strict supervision.

Now I can enter at will.

Avoiding the center of the room, I search the shelves and drawers for what I will need. Adrenaline pumps through me as I make my plans. My ears ring and my chest grows tight.

This time it will not go wrong.

This time it will work.

TEN

RYLAN FLYNN

The full moon fills the night sky as I drive to Aunt Val's. Music blares, gearing me up for what we are about to do. I sing at the top of my lungs along with Nine Inch Nails. The music works. As I pull in and park next to Dad's Taurus, my blood is pumping with anticipation at talking to the ghost that died in these woods last night.

I put the Caddy in park and turn off the music. The quiet of the night descends, broken by Mickey's car pulling in behind me. We climb out together. She's holding the video camera.

Mickey looks up at the moon. "Nice night for ghost hunting," she says.

"Every night is a good night for ghosts," I reply, looking up at the starry sky above the clearing.

"Up here," Dad says from the porch. George sees Mickey and me and bounds down the steps. He puts his big paws on my chest, begging for attention.

"George, that's enough," Val says, snapping her fingers at the dog.

George sticks his nose in my face for a final greeting then runs back up the porch steps.

"How does this work?" Val asks as we join her and Dad.

"I thought it would be best if we go to the place where we found her."

"But it's a crime scene," Val protests.

"We won't go into the scene. We'll stay outside of the tape, right?" Dad says, worried. "The police would have a fit if they knew we were doing this, let alone if we breached the tape."

"You ask her questions and I will help her pass over when you're done," Dad says. I don't like the shake of nerves in his voice. He's done this twice before with me, but never for a murder victim. A grandma in the attic is a different story from this.

I look at Mickey, who's shifting her weight from foot to foot. "Ready?" I ask her.

"Let me put George up," Val says opening her front door and ushering the dog inside.

"You're coming?" I ask in surprise.

"Wouldn't miss you at work. This is the most excitement I've had in a long time."

"Okay." I lead everyone off the porch and into the woods. Dad has a flashlight, but the moon is so bright it's not really needed.

"I think it was over this way," I say, crunching through the underbrush. I keep my eyes peeled for the young woman in the red T-shirt, but she doesn't show herself.

We walk without talking until we see the crime tape fluttering. "There it is," I whisper into the night.

"Oh, that poor thing," Dad says, eyeing the tree that is now empty.

Mickey raises the camera to her shoulder. "How do you want to do this? The usual?"

I nod, then smooth my hair into place behind my shoulders. I turn to the camera when Mickey is ready. "This is Rylan Flynn with *Beyond the Dead*. We are in the woods of Indiana, investigating a ghost that I saw here earlier today. The young woman was murdered here last night and she found me this morning. She led me to her body."

Something flickers behind Val, drawing my attention. I flick my eyes at Dad and he turns around slowly to face the flicker.

"Don't be scared," I tell the shape. The shadow takes form and steps toward me.

"She's here," I whisper to the camera. Mickey moves the camera to point where I am staring into the dark. Leaves crunch, although no one takes a step.

"Did you hear that?" Mickey asks the group.

The spirit cocks her head and opens her mouth. A strangled sound comes out of her lips.

"Don't try to talk. I know something is in there."

She nods, frantically trying to communicate. She puts her hands to her throat.

"Good. That's good. Just nod or shake your head."

The spirit locks eyes with mine. She nods slowly, understanding. I flick my eyes to Mickey, making sure she is taping the whole thing. Although, of course, she's only hearing my half of the conversation.

"She agrees," I tell the camera. "Let's see what we can find out. Let's start with the most basic question." I turn back to the ghost. "Do you know you are dead?"

Her eyes grow wide in confusion and she claws at her throat again. She shakes her head violently, not wanting to face the truth.

"She's upset," I say.

"I'm so sorry, dear," Dad says. "You were murdered last night."

The ghost's eyes dart to Dad and back to me. "She hears you," I say to Dad.

"Did he do this to you?" I ask the ghost, pointing to the cuts on her legs and arms.

She holds out her arms as if she just realized they were cut, then looks at me in question. "Did the man that killed you cut you?" I ask again.

She pushes her lips together and tries to talk, nodding her head.

I'm not surprised.

"Do you know the man who did this to you?" I push.

She shakes her head and scrunches her face, trying to tell me more, to make me understand.

"Okay. Let's try something else. Do you know who tied you to the tree?" I point to the tree where I found her. She follows my gesture, a pained look crossing her features.

She nods "yes" and walks through the tape toward the tree.

"She's walking to the tree," I say for the benefit of the camera. Mickey pans in that direction.

The ghost raises a hand and touches the bark, her eyes wide.

"Do you remember?" I ask from behind the tape.

She slowly shakes her head. She seems mesmerized.

Then she snaps out of it and suddenly runs straight at me.

It takes all of my experience not to flinch or duck.

She stops just inches away. Her mouth opens and she makes a strangled sound. She coughs and gags.

I hold my ground, not wanting her to know how scared I am with her so close.

She bends over her hands and wretches. When she rights herself, there is something in her hand, glittering in the moonlight.

"I did it," she says, holding up a coin. She stares at the coin and turns it over in her palm. It has a triangle pointing up on one side and another triangle pointing down on the other. There are extra lines at the base of the triangles. She flips it several times, then the coin disappears.

"I can talk," she says, her voice hoarse. Her eyes meet mine and questions fill my mind. I open my mouth to ask them, but she begins to fade.

"No, don't go," I plead.

Her face fills with panic and she looks at her arms as they turn to shadow.

"She's passing over," Dad says. "I can feel the shift in the air. Lord, accept this child into your arms and comfort her soul."

I whip around to face the three of them. "But she can talk now. She choked up a coin."

When I turn back to her, her mouth is open wide, but no sound comes out. A light opens up behind her, brighter than the moon. She looks over her shoulder at the light, then back at me in question.

"Go toward it. It's okay," I tell her.

I hear Dad praying softly. The girl turns and takes a step into the brightness. It consumes her, then she's gone.

Gone.

The woods fall quiet after she disappears.

"What happened?" Val whispers into the silence.

"She crossed over," I say miserably. "She's gone."

"Her soul is at rest now," Dad tries to console me.

"But we didn't learn anything useful." I want to wail, to cry, to curse God for taking her before I got any answers.

"God told you what he needs you to know," Dad says.

I twist my fingers in my hair in agitation. "I'm not in the mood for that right now. I was so close to getting an answer. Imagine solving a murder by talking to the victim."

"Your calling isn't to solve murders," Dad says gently. "Your calling is to help the souls that get stuck here."

I suddenly remember the camera that Mickey has trained on my face. I switch out of pouting mode and into host mode. "Well, folks. That was quite the interaction. She was here and tried to communicate. In the end, she disappeared." I don't know what else to say. "This is Rylan Flynn with *Beyond the*

Dead signing off." I look away from the camera and into the woods, hoping for a last glimpse of the girl, although I know it's not going to happen.

The woods are quiet. We can't even hear traffic, although I know the road isn't too far from here. This is a perfect place to commit a murder.

The young woman chose me to help her. Now I just have to figure out how to catch the man who chose this spot.

ELEVEN

RYLAN FLYNN

"What happens now?" Aunt Val asks as we stand near the crime scene, the yellow tape fluttering in the dark.

"We've done all we can," Dad says.

"Usually we have to help the spirit find the light. This time the light came for her," I say.

"Did you see it?" Mickey asks in a soft voice. "You really saw the light that took her?"

"I saw the light, but not what is behind it. I can't see the other side, only the spirits that are stuck." I poke at the leaves with the toe of my sneaker, despondent. I really wanted more from this encounter.

Val reaches for my hand and gives it a squeeze. She looks like she wants to say something. Instead, she drops my hand and turns away. "Let's get back. This place is starting to freak me out a bit."

We follow her through the woods and back to the cabin, my mind racing with what to do next.

"What are you going to do?" Dad asks, as if he read my mind.

"I don't know for sure. I should probably call Ford and tell

him that she says she didn't know the man that killed her but
did know who tied her to the tree. More than one person must
be involved. That might be some help. I could also tell him
about the coin." Val opens the door to the cabin and George
bounds out, sniffing us each in turn. I absently pet his wide
black head. "I'm not sure he will want to hear what I have to
say."

"Yeah, he wasn't too happy with us last night," Mickey
says.

"And that wasn't a crime scene," I say.

"But we didn't go under the tape," Dad offers.

"I'm not sure he'll care about that distinction," I say.

I check my phone surprised it's not later. It feels like a long
time since we went into the woods. "I wonder if he's up."

"With a murderer on the loose, I doubt he's at home sleeping," Val says.

"Worth a try." I pull up his number and hit call.

He doesn't pick up and my mind races with what to say as a
message. When the beep comes, I stumble over my words.
"Hey, Ford, this is Rylan. I, um, I have some information you
might need. Um, I know it's late. Call me if you get this.
Thanks, bye."

I hang up and find Mickey staring at me with a knowing
look. "Smooth," she teases.

"Oh, shut up."

"I, for one, am ready to go home," Dad says. He struggles to
hide a yawn. I remember that he's an early riser, not used to
late-night ghost hunts. "You be careful. Don't go chasing after
this guy on your own. Tell Ford what you know and leave it to
him."

I tell him I will, but he gives me a look that says he doesn't
believe me.

"What?" I ask, feigning innocence.

He shakes his head and walks down the steps to his car.

"Call me tomorrow and tell me how it goes." I raise a hand and wave goodbye.

"So," Mickey says, "Is that it for tonight?"

"I guess so. I don't know what else we can do now."

"Go home and get some rest. This has been a really long day for you."

"I will," I lie. I'm tired, but I don't feel up to facing my house right now. Besides, I checked online earlier, and the band, Loose Gravel, is playing at The Lock Up tonight. I'm hoping to catch the end of their show and see if I can find out if they know who the dead girl is.

I still don't even know her name.

Mickey and I make our goodbyes to Val and George and she follows me down the steps. "You're not going home, are you?" Mickey asks.

"Nope," I say. "Not when there is a killer out there. This girl came to me. I'm involved now."

"Want me to come with you?" I can tell she'd rather go home to Marco.

"I can handle it. I'm just going to The Lock Up for a bit. What can happen?"

"With you, there's no telling," Mickey teases and climbs into her car. "Let's do the editing tomorrow on this," she says, motioning to the camera. "Hopefully, the footage doesn't disappear again. I'll go home and back it up right now."

"Sounds good." I stand in the clearing and watch her drive down the lane. Val goes inside with George and I'm alone under the full moon, which fills the clearing with light. I look to the moon and close my eyes.

"Lord, guide me where you need me," I pray to the sky. My phone rings, interrupting my moment.

My blood tingles when I see it is Ford returning my call. "Hello, this is Rylan," I answer.

"Hey, Ry, I got your message." His voice is smooth and

deep. I can hear music and talking in the background. "What did you need to tell me about Celeste's murder?"

"Is that her name, Celeste?"

He hesitates a moment. "Yes. Celeste Monroe. You had something to tell me?"

I listen to the loud music on his end. "Are you at The Lock Up? Is that Loose Gravel playing?"

Ford sighs. "Yes. Why?"

"I was just headed there." I pull open my driver's door and settle into the big car. "Stay there and we can talk."

The music plays a few bars before he answers. "Fine. I'll wait."

He sounds annoyed, but then he usually sounds that way. He's probably just tired. "Be there in ten," I say and hang up before he can change his mind.

I turn up the music and jam out again as I make my way to the bar. My traitorous heart thumps knowing I'll be talking to Ford in a few minutes.

I shake my head in disgust. "Honestly, Ry," I say to myself, using the nickname Ford used. "This is a murder investigation, not a date."

A date.

Someday.

Music fills the parking lot when I park outside the bar a few minutes later. I check my face and hair in the rearview mirror. The parking lot is dark except for the moon. Even in the gloom I look pale. I dig through my purse, looking for lipstick or a stray eyeliner. I'm not surprised when my search turns up nothing that will make me look better. I settle for pinching my cheeks until they have some color.

"Holy flip, stop being so self-conscious. It's just Ford. It's nothing," I tell my reflection and push the door open.

The one light that should be on in the parking lot is out and I'm thankful for the moon as I cross the gravel behind the bar. I keep my eyes on the ground, not wanting to see if there are any spirits out here. A dark parking lot is a good place for them to sneak up on me.

As I approach the door, a couple pour out into the night. The woman is laughing and falls into me. Her long braid smacks me in the face as she tumbles. The man puts his arm around her waist and helps her up. "Sorry," she mumbles, smiling, a dimple deep in one cheek. Once back on her feet, they both laugh and keep walking. I hope they are not driving. I watch them cross the parking lot and walk toward the front of the building. I wait for the sound of a car starting, but don't hear anything. I imagine they must be walking home and put them out of my mind.

I pull open the door to the bar and walk inside. The music envelopes me and I find myself nodding my head to the beat. A crowd has surrounded the band, swaying and gyrating to the heavy beat, their hands raised toward the music. I watch the lead singer, wondering if he knows Celeste. He reaches to touch the hand of a girl in the front row who looks vaguely familiar.

"I see you made it," Ford says near my ear, startling me. He's so close I can feel his breath on my neck.

I turn and meet his crisp blue eyes. "So I did." My heart is beating as fast as the music.

"Want a drink?" I notice he is not wearing the blue polo that he wore to the crime scene this morning. He's in a black T-shirt that clings to his chest.

"I'd love a vodka tonic." I tuck a strand of hair behind my ear and follow him to the bar.

"Are you off duty?" I ask after he places my order with a cute, blond bartender.

"Sort of. I'm here to talk to the drummer and I figured I'd get further if I wasn't dressed as a cop."

"Smart." I nod. "I had the same idea. Celeste had this band's shirt on. I wondered if they knew her."

Ford stares at me. "Why?"

"Why what?"

"Why are you looking into the case? That is my job. There's something, maybe several somethings, you're not telling me." He reaches behind my ear and I resist the urge to lean into his hand. He pulls something from my hair and shows it to me. It's a small twig. "Been in the woods?" he asks, his eyes narrowing further.

The bartender hands me my drink. I busy myself with squeezing the lime into the glass instead of answering. Ford takes what looks like a Coke from the girl behind the bar and gives her a dazzling smile. "Thank you," he tells her.

"Coke's on the house, detective," she says, then looks at me for payment, her smile not reaching her eyes now. I dig a few bills out of my purse and hand them over. Her eyes linger on Ford as she turns toward the register.

"Looks like you have a fan," I say.

Ford seems surprised. "Oh? I hadn't noticed. Now stop trying to change the subject. This?" He still holds the small twig.

I stall by taking a sip of my drink, enjoying the bitter bite of the tonic and lime. "Okay, so I wasn't totally honest with you about how I found the body this morning," I finally say.

"I figured as much."

"Full truth is the ghost of Celeste Monroe came to find me while I was sitting on Aunt Val's porch. She beckoned me to follow her, so I did."

Ford leans on the bar, his attention focused on me. "She came to you?"

I nod and continue. "I followed her to the tree and then she disappeared. I didn't want to get into all that with the police, with you, this morning. So I said George found her."

The band ends the song and starts up another one. Ford is quiet.

"You saw the ghost of a murder victim and didn't tell me?"

"That's not all." I take another long suck on my straw, stalling. "I talked to her again after we went back to the cabin. Well, she tried to talk, but she had something stuck in her throat."

Ford straightens. "In her throat?"

"Wait, I'm not done." I look at the band and sip again. I really don't want to tell him what we did tonight, what I saw.

"Go on," he says. From his tone, I once again feel like a suspect being questioned.

"Tonight, Dad, Mickey, Val and I went into the woods."

"Tell me you didn't go into the crime scene." He bristles.

"No. Not into it, just outside of the tape. We went there to try to communicate with her again. Dad came to help her cross over to the next realm."

"Fine. What did you learn? You said you had information."

"When I asked her if she knew the man that killed her, she shook her head vehemently. She didn't know him."

"Or it wasn't a him," he says.

I sip again, thinking on that. "Could be. She led me to believe that one person killed her but another tied her. She said no to knowing the man that killed her but yes to knowing who tied her to the tree."

"Interesting. What else?"

"The other thing is the coin."

He is all attention now. "Coin?"

"She had a coin stuck in her throat and she coughed it up when we were with her. I saw it for a moment. It had a triangle with a line through it on one side and the same thing but upside down on the other."

Ford reaches into his pocket and pulls out his phone. He brings up a picture. "Like this?"

The screen shows the coin I saw in Celeste's hand. "Yes, exactly like that. Where did you get that picture?"

"Coroner Marrero found it in her throat during the autopsy. It's what killed her." He studies my face.

"Do you know what it is? What the markings are?"

"Working on it." He sips his Coke, thinking. "You really saw her, didn't you?"

I try not to take offense. I've known Ford since we were kids, and he's known about my abilities for years. This is the first time he has asked me directly about it.

"Did you think I was faking it all this time?"

He stiffens. "Not that you were faking it, but seeing a hazy form in an old house and actually talking to a murder victim are two very different things."

"Well, I don't always see them so clearly. This was a little different, I'll admit," I say, calming down.

"What else did you learn? Did she talk once the coin was out of her throat?"

I shake my head. "Sadly, she was taken by the light before I could get anything else out of her."

Ford takes a long drink from his Coke. He finally looks me in the eye. "You saw the light?"

"That's the same thing Mickey asked. I've seen it lots of times. That's what I do the most. I try to help the lost spirits cross over. It's not all about getting an encounter on tape. That's just how I pay the bills."

He stares over the rim of his plastic cup. "I always thought *Beyond the Dead* was the only thing you did."

I'm surprised he used the name of my show. "Have you seen our channel?"

He looks over my shoulder. "Maybe a few episodes. I need to know what buildings you are trespassing in."

"We are normally invited," I point out. "Clients call me from all over."

He seems impressed. "Interesting."

His focus shifts behind me. A man has approached the bar. "Phew, finally done," he says to the bartender. "Can I get a shot of Fireball?"

It's the lead singer, and the rest of the band soon join him at the bar. I had been so involved in talking to Ford, I hadn't noticed the band finishing up their last set. The group is full of long hair and sweaty T-shirts. They look tired, but buzzed with the excitement of being on stage. I've watched this band a few times before and am a little star-struck at being so close to them.

"Back to work," Ford says, his shoulders straightening, his muscles moving under his T-shirt. I pull my eyes away from his chest and step back so he can continue the investigation.

TWELVE

RYLAN FLYNN

I lean against the bar and watch Ford work.

"Hey," Ford says to the group as they pick up their round of shots.

The lead singer looks at him and holds up his shot glass. Without a word he downs the liquid in one gulp. The others behind him do the same. The singer wipes his lips with the back of his hand and sets the shot glass on the bar.

"Is this about that girl, Celeste?" the singer asks.

"Why do you think that?"

"You're obviously a cop and word is she was murdered last night."

Ford scans the group crowding behind the singer. "I understand she dated your drummer." He focuses on a thin man with long, even thinner hair.

The man steps forward, his expression grim. "That's me. Celeste was my girl, I guess."

"You're Drew? You don't seem all that shook up about her death," Ford points out.

"I was in rehearsal all day and then came to the show tonight. I didn't find out until one of the girls told me on our first break." He looks away, his eyes growing red and his face flushing. "I haven't had time to think about her." He suddenly looks Ford down. "That doesn't mean I didn't care about her. She moved here to be with me. If she had stayed in Toledo, this wouldn't have happened."

Ford keeps his composure. "Were you and Celeste having any problems lately? Moving to Ashby was a big change for her, bound to be some tension."

Drew wipes at his eyes. "You cops are all the same. Must be the boyfriend, right? I didn't have anything to do with it. I cared for Celeste and would never have hurt her."

The rest of the band is watching intently, especially the woman with short dark hair I recognize as the bass player.

The woman steps forward. "Besides, Drew was with us last night." She lifts her chin in challenge.

Ford pins her with his eyes. "Is that right? He was with you all night?"

"Not with me, exactly, but at the house. We were all there."

Ford looks at the rest of the group. "You all can vouch for him?"

The group nods in unison.

Drew looks relieved. "I told you I didn't have anything to do with her death."

Ford steps back and takes a sip of his Coke. "Okay. You know I have to ask the questions. It's nothing personal."

Drew looks at the ground, his long hair swinging in front of his face. "I understand. Do whatever you have to do to find the killer. Just don't waste time with me." He lifts his head. "Or the band."

A blond woman suddenly cuts in front of Ford and leans into the lead singer. It's the same blond that he was reaching for while singing earlier. I still get the vague feeling that I know her. She's obviously been drinking as she sways on her feet.

"Steady, there," the singer says, holding her by the upper arms.

"You were amazing tonight." There is a slight slur to her words. "Buy me a drink?"

"I don't think you are old enough for a drink, Kimmie Steele," Ford says.

Then I realize why she looks so familiar. She's the girl that works for Val at The Hole sometimes. She looks different with her hair down and not wearing the donut-shop apron.

Kimmie spins unsteadily and narrows her eyes at Ford. "Oh no, Detective Pierce."

"I think it's time you found a ride home," Ford tells her.

"I have a ride." Kimmie scans the room. "Tabitha," she calls loudly across the bar.

A plump girl with limp hair joins the group. She darts her eyes at Ford and me and then looks at the ground.

"See, Tabitha is sober as can be. She's my designated tonight," Kimmie says.

"Neither of you are old enough to be in bars yet," Ford points out.

"Not according to the ID in my pocket," Kimmie says saucily.

Ford rolls his eyes and holds out his hand.

"Seriously," Kimmie says, digging into her too-tight jeans. She pulls out an ID and slaps it in Ford's palm. Tabitha does the same.

Kimmie suddenly turns her attention on me. "What are you looking at?" she demands. She leans in so close I can smell beer on her breath. "Wait, I know you. You're my boss's niece. You come to the shop a lot."

"I'm Rylan," I say, trying to be polite. After all, the girl did just lose her friend in a horrible way.

"You're the ghost hunter," Kimmie says.

"Among other things," I answer and take another sip of my almost-empty drink.

Kimmie looks me up and down, and I fight the urge to smooth my hair under her scrutiny. "Why are you here? Are you investigating Celeste's murder, too? Some kind of consultant? Let me guess, Celeste's ghost talked to you."

I'm shocked that she's right.

"She did," I concede.

"Cool," the lead singer says. "You see ghosts and work with the police?"

"She's not a consultant," Ford cuts in with authority. "Tabitha, maybe you should take Kimmie home now."

Tabitha steps forward and gently leads Kimmie away. "Come on, Kimmie, you're obviously upset about Celeste and not thinking right. Plus, Mom needs me home."

This gets through Kimmie's drunkenness, and she collapses into Tabitha's arms.

"I'm just so upset about Celeste." She looks to Ford. "You will find the monster that took her, right?"

"Let's go," Tabitha says, soothing her friend.

With a forlorn look at the lead singer, Kimmie allows herself to be removed.

Ford goes back to work. "I'd like it if you could come down to the station tomorrow and give a formal statement about Celeste," he says to Drew.

Drew nods eagerly. "Of course, whatever you need that might help."

"Is that all?" the girl bass player asks. I notice she puts a hand on Drew's shoulder. She doesn't seem too upset by Celeste's death. I get the feeling she'll be more than happy to comfort Drew.

"That's all," Ford says. "For now." He drinks the rest of his Coke and sits the empty cup on the bar. "Rylan, you ready to go?"

I'm surprised he wants to leave with me. I finish my drink and follow him to the door, wishing we were leaving together, not just walking out at the same time.

The parking lot is lit only by the moon as I hurry to catch up to him.

"I see you're still driving your mom's old Cadillac."

"It's reliable and it gets me around town," I say, slightly embarrassed by the boat of a car.

"It's hard to miss you," he says, his eyes crinkling in the moonlight. He opens the door for me and I stand in the opening. "Can't imagine you get good gas mileage."

I don't want to talk about gas mileage, I want him to lean over and kiss me.

A fool's wish.

"It does okay," I say lamely, wanting the moment to stretch.

"Well, I don't suppose it will do any good, but I feel I need to point out that working this case is my job, not yours. You need to stay away.

Any illusions of romance disappear.

"But Celeste came to me for help. She needs me."

"Rylan, Celeste is dead. Her ghost may have come to you, but she is gone. I work for the dead."

"So do I." I lift my chin.

He looks away in suppressed anger. "Just stay out of my case."

"You stay out of mine and we'll get along just fine." I want the words back as soon as they leave my mouth.

"Your case?"

"The ghost of Celeste and what she wants is my case."

"Then go make your show, but leave the police work to me and Tyler."

"But I can help. I did help."

He runs a hand over his face in agitation. "There's no

winning with you, is there? You're going to poke your nose where it doesn't belong regardless of what I say."

"I'll do what I need to do, and I won't break the law."

"You did last night by trespassing at the Morton Manor. You could have gotten hurt in that mess of a place."

He has me there. "That's different. That place has been abandoned for years. You should see all the empty beer bottles and stuff inside. Lots of people sneak in there."

"Right. Other trespassers."

"Ghosts don't usually hang out in public places," I point out.

He blows out air, irritated. "Just stay out of Celeste's case."

"Fine." I hate that I don't have a wittier comeback. I retreat into the car.

"I mean it," he says, leaning into the open door.

"I know." I pull the door shut. He has to back away quickly when I start the car and put it in reverse. I wave my fingers and pull out of the parking spot. I can't stop myself from watching him in the rearview mirror.

"Holy flip, that was a mess," I say to Ford's reflection. This is two nights in a row I've driven away from him.

"Stupid, stupid, stupid," I chastise myself as I drive home. "Next time try not to be so awkward."

A deep tired envelopes me as I park in my driveway and walk to my front door. I fumble with the handle and push the door open. The musty smell of home fills my nostrils, and my many belongings surround me in comfort.

"Honey, I'm home," I say sarcastically, half expecting Mom to answer. When I check her room, she isn't there. I'm a bit relieved. I've had my fill of the beyond for the day.

I skirt around the door to the other bedroom and slip into mine.

With a huge yawn, I kick off my shoes and fall onto the crowded bed.

"Lord, please accept Celeste into your arms," I pray. "And help us find her killer," I add as sleep slides over me.

Sometime later, I hear a noise in the hall. I've woken to this noise before. A knocking on Keaton's childhood bedroom door echoes through the house.

"Not tonight," I whisper, pulling my pillow over my head. "Go away."

The knocking grows louder.

Desperate, I take out one of the sets of headphones I keep in my drawer. I pull them on and link the Bluetooth from my phone. I queue up a song list and turn the volume way up.

The music almost drowns out the pounding in the hall.

Almost.

THIRTEEN

FORD PIERCE

I dream of Rylan.

Shattered images and flashes of visions. In all of them, she is torn and bloody. In all of them, she is surrounded by spirits. Not vague shadows, but fully formed bodies. They pull at her, tear her clothes, slice her skin like someone did to Celeste.

She reaches out for help. I try to run to her, but spirits hold my feet to the ground. I kick at them, but cannot escape.

She is pulled into a hole of red light.

I scream her name.

And wake in a sweat.

It takes me several moments to realize I am in my own bed. That I'm alone.

Since I left my fiancé, Kaitlyn, a few months ago, sleeping alone seems strange.

It takes several more minutes until my heart stops pounding.

"Just a dream, stop being so dramatic." I throw the blankets off in disgust at myself and sit on the edge of the bed. My head aches and my neck is stiff. I check the time on my phone. I've only been asleep for a few hours.

I don't feel rested, but I get up anyway. There's a killer in my town and I will find him.

And keep Rylan out of it. Keep her safe.

Later at our office, Tyler looks as if he didn't fare much better in the sleep department than I did.

"You look like crap," he says when I sit at my desk.

"Yeah, so do you."

He leans back in his chair and stretches his arms over his head. "I offered to go to the bar with you," he reminds me. "How did it go?"

"I talked to the band and to her boyfriend, Drew. This doesn't feel like a boyfriend losing his temper kind of murder. Too ritualistic."

"Unless he was into that kind of thing."

"I don't think he had anything to do with it. Plus, his housemates swear they were together all night."

"So a dead end. Unless he snuck out or something."

"Yeah, I don't think so." I take a drink of my coffee. "Was an interesting night, though. You'll never guess who showed up at the bar."

Tyler studies my face. "I bet it was Rylan Flynn."

"How'd you know?" I nearly knock my coffee over in surprise.

Tyler leans back again. "I'm a good detective."

"Not that good."

"You look like you've been beat up last night. You often look like that when you have a run-in with her." Tyler wears a self-satisfied smile.

"No I don't."

He shrugs. "Okay, if you say so. It's simple deduction. She found the body and she's nosey. She probably wanted to talk to the band on Celeste's shirt."

I'm impressed and a little annoyed.

"She did. How did you...?"

Tyler suddenly laughs out loud. "Stop looking so surprised. My friend saw her there talking to you and the band last night. Said there were tons of people at the bar. I guess it got out about Celeste wearing that band's T-shirt and people got curious." He grins, like he pulled a great joke on me. "I'm good, but I'm not psychic like she is."

"She's not psychic, she sees ghosts."

"Isn't that the same thing?"

"Not exactly. She can't tell the future or anything like that."

Tyler studies my face again. "Uh-huh," he says enigmatically.

"I don't want to talk about Rylan. That girl gives me a headache." I rub at my temple where my head still pounds after my nightmare. "What time are we meeting Celeste's mom at her apartment?"

"In about an hour." Tyler flips through the file on his desk. "What do we know about the coin Marrero found?"

"Nothing yet. Hopefully we can figure out what the triangles mean. There has to be a reason it was in her throat. That combined with the cuts definitely make this look like some kind of ritual."

"Whoever did this was obviously disturbed."

I debate telling Tyler what Rylan did last night. I can't keep something so big from my partner. "According to Rylan, Celeste either didn't know her killer or it wasn't a man."

Tyler looks up from the papers. "According to Rylan?"

I swallow, suddenly feeling foolish. It's a struggle for me to understand what she does, and I don't think Tyler is as open-minded as I am. I've had years to get used to her unusual ways. Tyler barely knows her.

"She went into the woods to talk to Celeste's ghost."

Tyler sits up straight. "Did she talk to her?" he asks excitedly. I'm surprised.

"I didn't think you believed in that kind of thing."

He darts his eyes at the door, then says in a low voice. "Have you seen her show? She's the real thing."

"I have seen an episode or two," I lie. I've actually seen every one. There's something quite compelling about them.

"What else did Celeste tell her?"

"Not much. She had that coin stuck in her throat so she couldn't talk. Then she was taken to the other side."

"Did she tape it?" He's sitting on the edge of his seat. "Was Mickey Ramirez with her?"

"I think so. Mickey and Rylan's dad."

"Did you see the one where her dad prays over a spirit and they help him cross over?"

I nod. "That one's a bit creepy."

Tyler sits back, satisfied. "If she can talk to victims that would make our job easier."

"I don't think it works that way."

"No? Too bad Celeste's spirit is gone. We could use some help on this one."

"We can solve it the way we solve every other case. Good police work."

"Imagine. She could say, 'Who killed you?' and they could tell us."

"If it worked like that, she'd find the ghost of her mother and ask her who shot her in the head."

Tyler grows sober. "I suppose you're right. Margie Flynn's would be the first case she would solve. Maybe her mom isn't a ghost so she can't ask her."

"Enough talk about Rylan." An image of her torn and bloodied and surrounded by dark spirits pops into my mind. "Let's go meet Celeste's mom at her apartment. There must be something useful there."

. . .

Celeste's apartment is on the first floor of an old house that was turned into a duplex at some point. A woman sits on the steps leading to the front porch. She stares at her feet, her head bowed in sadness.

Celeste's mother.

My heart aches for the woman. I can't even imagine the hell she must be living through right now.

Mrs. Monroe lifts her head as we approach. I expect to see tears, but her eyes are dry.

"Detectives," she says in greeting, her voice steady.

"I'm Detective Pierce. We spoke on the phone yesterday."

"Right." She gives a small nod to Tyler. "That makes you Spencer."

"It does. Thank you for coming. We really need to know if anything looks out of place or is missing."

Mrs. Monroe stands and brushes off her rear with agitated swipes. "I'm not sure I'm the right person to tell you about my daughter. That girl has been a wild child since she was born. I'm not sure I even knew her at all."

Strange words from a grieving mother.

"Well, anything you can tell us will be useful," I say.

She gives me a stern look. "It won't bring her back."

I mentally flinch. "No, it won't. But, hopefully, it can tell us what happened, and who did this to her."

She crosses her arms on her chest. "I heard she was tied to a tree. Is that true?"

I'm the one who told her yesterday, but I don't mind telling her again. "It is."

She shakes her head and her shoulders sag. "That doesn't make sense."

"Why's that?"

"Celeste was not what you'd call the outdoors type. I don't understand why she'd be in the woods at all."

"She was most likely taken there against her will," I point out.

She looks at the ground and runs her foot along a crack in the sidewalk. "I suppose that's true." She suddenly lifts her head, and her voice is stern again. "Let's get this over with." She turns and stomps up the steps, pulling a key out of her pocket.

The key is unnecessary; the door is slightly ajar.

I look at Tyler and we both go on alert. "Please step over there," Tyler tells Mrs. Monroe, as he pulls out his gun and holds it at the ready.

I press a hand on the wood door, my own gun prepared. "Police," I call into the apartment. "If someone is in there, you'd better come out."

The apartment is quiet and dim. I press my back to the outside wall and peer into the gloom, looking for any sign of movement.

"What's going on?" Mrs. Monroe says in a loud whisper. "Is someone in there?"

After checking the small, sparsely furnished living room, I step inside the apartment. Adrenaline pumps through my veins, my senses on high alert. "Hello. Police."

It is so quiet inside that I can hear the refrigerator humming. Tyler follows close behind. We clear the living room and the kitchen area, then move down the short hall.

The bathroom door is half open and I quickly check it out. I even pull the red shower curtain back to make sure no one is hiding there.

"Police. If someone is in here, its best you come out now," Tyler says as he turns the knob on the closed bedroom door.

The door flies open and a figure pummels into the hall, pushing Tyler aside. The young man tries to run past me, but there is no room in the hall. I grab him by the long hair and toss him to the floor.

"Why are you here?" I demand, as I place cuffs on him to keep him detained.

"I didn't mean anything," he says, squirming into a seated position.

"Did you know Celeste?" Tyler asks.

The man pants a few breaths, nodding. "You're the guitarist from Loose Gravel, aren't you?" I say. "I saw you play last night."

"Yeah. I am."

"You weren't with them when I talked to the band after the show."

"I had to get out of there. It was all I could do to play the sets after I heard what happened to Celeste."

"Why's that? How well did you know her?" Tyler asks. "I thought she was dating the drummer."

The man makes a sound of disgust. "Drew. He dates all the girls. He didn't know what he had in Celeste."

"So you knew her well?" I ask.

The man looks up. "I loved her."

"Why are you here?" I repeat.

He hangs his head, his long hair covering his face. "To get the, you know," he mutters, barely audible.

"We don't know. Why don't you tell us," Tyler says, leaning over the man.

He raises his head, his face red. "The condom. I came to get it from the trash. I watch TV. I know how the DNA stuff works. You guys find that and test it you'd know about me and Celeste. Then I'd be a suspect."

"You and Celeste were having an affair?" I ask.

"It wasn't an affair. It was love."

"So you were in love. What did Drew have to say about that?" Tyler asks.

He swings his hair out of his eyes. "He didn't know. She was going to tell him, but..."

"She didn't get the chance," Tyler supplies.

"Right." His voice cracks. "Now she's gone."

"If Drew knew about you two, he could have taken revenge on her," Tyler says.

"Maybe. But I really don't think he knew. If he does, he hides it well."

Tyler and I exchange looks, then I help the man onto his feet and remove his cuffs. "What's your name?"

"Andy Wells."

"Andy, we'll need you to come down to the station and make a full statement about Celeste and your relationship with her."

"Our relationship? Really? Can't we keep this between us? Drew will throw a fit and that will make things messy with the band."

"Maybe you should have thought about that before," Tyler says.

"Where were you two nights ago?" I ask as I put the cuffs back on my belt.

"I was home with the band all night. We practiced some, then we had a few drinks then went to bed. I'm sure they could all vouch for me."

"So Drew was there all night and so were you?" I ask.

"Yes. That's right."

"One of you could have snuck out to meet her and things went astray," I say.

"But I didn't. I was there all night."

"We'll check that out," I say and let him go. "We'll have more questions for you."

"Safe to come in?" Mrs. Monroe looks through from the open front door.

"It's safe, but give us a moment."

"Who is this? Why did you break into Celeste's apartment?"

Andy looks to me for help. "This is Celeste's mom," I tell him.

An odd look crosses his face, then is replaced by a look of concern. "I'm sorry for your loss. I loved your daughter, too."

"Are you Drew? You're the one that lured her out here. Now she's dead." Her voice rises with emotion.

"I'm not Drew," he says tightly. "I'm Andy."

"I don't understand. She never mentioned an Andy."

"I'm sort of new," he says, his face burning red. "Am I free to go now?" he asks me.

"For now. But we'll want to talk to you again."

"No problem." With that, Andy Wells disappears out the door.

"So Celeste had two boyfriends," Mrs. Monroe says. "Just like that girl. Never satisfied." She looks around the room with only a couch and a TV on a rickety table. "Phew. This place is a dump." She looks into the kitchen, her gaze lingering on the dirty dishes in the sink. She shakes her head. "Why would she want to live here when we have a perfectly lovely home back in Toledo?"

I don't have an answer for her, so I change the subject. "Is there anything that looks out of place to you?"

She motions around the room. "All of it. None of this looks like Celeste. I mean look at that sofa, it's worn out and dirty. I just don't understand any of it."

"Look in her room. Maybe something will stand out to you there," Tyler says.

She walks down the short hall and goes into the bedroom. "Now this looks more like it."

Tyler and I follow into the small room. The walls are bare except for a poster with odd symbols on it. The dresser and mirror are covered with candles and strange knick-knacks. "What is all this stuff?" I ask Mrs. Monroe.

"That's her witch stuff."

"Witch as in pointy hats and brooms?" Tyler asks.

She snaps her head and gives him a dirty look. "Not like that, but yes."

"Celeste was into the occult?" I ask.

"Very. It caused a lot of our troubles the last year or so."

I take a closer look at the poster with the symbols. Two of them are familiar from the coin. "Do you know what these are?"

"She had that hanging in her room at home. I never paid it much attention."

One of the symbols is of the triangle with the extra bottom line. The poster says "Air" under it. The similar triangle that is upside down says "Earth."

I pull up the picture of the coin and show it to Mrs. Monroe. "Does this look familiar?"

"Is that the coin she choked on?"

"It is," I say gently.

"Earth and air. Like on the poster."

"Right. But have you seen this before?"

Mrs. Monroe studies the picture, then sadly shakes her head. "I've never seen the coin. I've only seen the poster."

"Do you know what the poster means?" I ask.

"Means my daughter was into more things than I knew. Never could trust that girl. Looks like even her boyfriends couldn't trust her."

FOURTEEN

The moon will be full for another night. Tonight is the perfect time.

And I have the perfect girl. Mom would be proud of my choice.

Willing and clueless.

She'll never know what's coming.

Until it's too late.

"You must do a better job tonight," the voice says from the painting.

I stare at the eyes, the dark, evil eyes captured by the artist.

"Remember all you've learned," it continues.

"I won't let you down this time."

I step over the body on the floor and pick up my bag of tools. It's a small bag, nondescript.

A bag of dreams ready to come true.

FIFTEEN

RYLAN FLYNN

After my very late night in the woods and then at the bar, I sleep longer than I planned. I barely have time to shower and get to Mickey's without being late. I can tell as soon as I enter her home office that something is wrong.

"Don't tell me the footage from last night is gone," I say, full of worry.

Mickey looks stricken. "No. I backed that up and it's safe."

"So why do you look so upset?"

"Lindy is at it again."

Lindy Parker. My least favorite person in Ashby.

"What is it this time?"

"She posted a new podcast episode this morning. Want to guess who it's about?"

"Her favorite target, me?" In addition to working at the District Attorney's office with Keaton, Lindy runs a podcast that is dedicated to debunking ghost hunters, like Mickey and me, as well as any type of occult investigators. She has a huge following, one that Mickey and I only wish for. I don't get her appeal. Her show is mostly vague innuendos and unproven accusations with a heavy dose of fear mongering. A lot of people are into that.

Just my luck she also lives in Ashby. She's made it her mission to prove I'm a fake. Of course, she's failed so far, but not for lack of trying.

"You guessed it. It's pretty bad. She vaguely suggests that you are involved in the murder of Celeste Monroe."

A sudden flash of anger surges through me. "Involved? As in responsible for Celeste's death?"

"She doesn't come out and say it, but she mentions how coincidental it is that you found the body. Here let me pull it up for you."

Mickey cues up the show and I sink into a chair as I listen to Lindy talk about me and how I found Celeste.

"I wouldn't be surprised if Rylan Flynn posts an episode where she 'talks' to the poor dead girl's ghost," Lindy says at one point. "Especially since she found the body."

I sit back in my chair, disgusted. "Now what?"

"What do you mean?"

"She's kind of right. If we post what we got last night, it will just give her more fuel against me."

"You've never let that stop us before."

"This is different. We usually deal with spirits that have been dead for a long time or that we don't know the identity of. Celeste has a family with raw wounds. I don't want to add to their pain with our feud with Lindy."

Mickey twirls a piece of her curly brown hair. "I suppose you are right, but what we got last night was gold."

"If Celeste was your sister or your friend, would you want her murder to be talked about on two shows?"

Mickey sits back in her chair. "So Lindy wins?"

"Lindy never wins. Let's just sit on the footage until it's not such a hot topic. Maybe we'll use it later. I don't want Lindy feeding off of Celeste's murder. If we don't talk about it that gives her nothing to discuss."

"Okay, I can go along with that. We still don't have the new episode then, and we are running out of time. We might lose a few followers if we don't give them something good."

I have an idea and I smile at Mickey. "Let's go back to Morton. The Morton Mistress might talk to me again and we can use that."

"We were banned from there."

"Exactly. So Officer Frazier won't be expecting us to go back."

"Or we could return one of the calls we've gotten from actual clients," Mickey says. "There are lots of requests for our services in my inbox. There's no shortage of strange happenings for us to investigate."

"We both know most of those turn out not to be real. The Morton Mistress is real."

"I'm in if you are."

The time of night is the same. The abandoned hallway with the crooked exit sign is the same. Even the full moon is the same.

But the Morton Mistress doesn't come.

"It's Rylan," I shout into the gloom of the hospital. Mickey has the camera focused on me as I walk around the hospital hallway. Last time doors slammed and the Mistress was eager to communicate.

There is nothing but an eerie silence now.

I look at the camera. "I guess she doesn't want to talk tonight." I give a rueful smile, knowing all this footage is probably not going to be used.

Mickey pans the camera away from me and around the hall. "Maybe she's somewhere else. Want to try downstairs?"

"Can't hurt."

Mickey turns off the camera and the light goes out. My eyes are not used to the dim and I can't see. I blink into the darkness. A sound rattles downstairs. "Did you hear that?"

"Of course, and I just turned the camera off," she grumbles and switches it back on. The sudden light is bright and I raise my hand to block it.

"We just heard a noise from downstairs," I tell the camera. "Hopefully, it is the Mistress."

"Whoever's up there, better not be Rylan Flynn and Mickey Ramirez," a voice bellows up the stairs and down the hall.

Mickey turns off the camera and the hall goes dark again. It's Officer Frazier in a cruel déjà vu of two nights ago. I want to duck into one of the many rooms and hide, but I fight the urge.

Mickey looks to me for guidance, her face barely visible in the dark.

"Rylan, I can't believe you," Frazier says, coming around the corner and shining his flashlight on us.

"You don't understand," I try.

"I understand you don't follow direct orders. You were told not to come here again. That meant ever."

"We lost all our footage from last time," Mickey says. "We had to come back."

"You had to stay away," Frazier says. He makes a sound of exasperation. "Rylan, what is it going to take? I should arrest you. Maybe then you'll get the hint."

"You can't arrest us," Mickey exclaims, her face full of fear. "Do something," she mouths to me.

Desperate, I try to find a way out. I can't let Mickey go to jail when this was my idea.

"You don't want to arrest me." I try for a slightly flirty tone, feeling slightly foolish. Back in middle school, Officer Frazier was just little Jimmy Frazier. He was a late bloomer and quiet. He also had a crush on me. He once sent me flowers at school.

The card said, "from your secret admirer," but I knew they were from him. It was humiliating. I wonder if he has any feelings left that could be worked to my advantage.

"I don't want to arrest you, but if that's what it will take to teach you a lesson."

There isn't a trace of little Jimmy Frazier in him.

"Come on, Jimmy," I try again, my voice as sweet and innocent as apple pie. "We don't have to go there."

"It's Officer James Frazier," he says stiffly, not impressed with my attempt at sweet talk. "Don't try that Jimmy stuff on me."

"But we didn't do anything, not really," I protest.

"Just trespassing and disobeying my direct orders." He puffs out his chest and removes his cuffs from his belt.

Mickey looks terrified. I have to do something.

"Just take me in and not Mickey," I beg.

"Fine. Then turn around and put your hands behind your back."

"No," Mickey says, jumping to my defense.

Panic surges through me. "You can't be serious."

"Try me." He steps forward, takes out his cuffs.

"You can't arrest her," Mickey protests.

"I can and I am. Warning hasn't worked. Now turn around."

I turn and put my hands behind my back in disbelief. I wonder if I should mention the flowers from eighth grade, but figure that will backfire.

"Don't do this," I plead.

He snaps one cuff on, the metal cold against my skin.

What will Keaton say?

Just then, his shoulder radio begins talking, loud in the abandoned hospital hall. "All available units to Belkin Road. Another body has been found."

Belkin Road. That's the road Aunt Val lives on.

Frazier responds to the call, then unsnaps my cuffs. "It's your lucky day," he says. "I have a bigger case to handle."

I rub my wrist and bite my tongue against a rude retort.

"They found another body?" Mickey asks.

"Don't you dare. You didn't hear anything. Go home and stay out of trouble." He hurries down the hall.

My phone vibrates in my pocket. I'm surprised, it's past midnight and no one usually calls me this late at night, except for maybe Mickey.

The caller ID shows it's Aunt Val. My stomach sinks. This can't be good.

"Rylan, I n-need you," Val says, without saying hello first. Her stutter doesn't go unnoticed.

"Where are you?"

"I'm at home. Well in the w-woods near h-home. George found her."

"Found who? Val, what is going on?"

"Just come. Please, Rylan. She m-might still be here. She might tell y-you what happened to her?"

I look at Mickey's questioning face, then say, "Mickey's with me. We'll be right there."

SIXTEEN

RYLAN FLYNN

"Should I bring the camera?" Mickey asks once we are parked at Aunt Val's. We passed several police cars and Coroner Marrero's van parked on the road. From the clearing at Val's house, we can see the lights of the vehicles glowing in the sky over the woods.

"Leave the camera here. We're not going to be welcome as it is."

Mickey eyes the lights in the sky. "Looks like the same place where Celeste was found."

"It does," I agree, bending to re-tie my sneaker. "Why does this keep happening on Val's property?"

"Poor Val. She must be so upset."

"Let's go find out." I tighten the bow on my Converse and head into the woods.

It doesn't take long to find the crime scene. The yellow tape is bright in the darkness, the lights of the crew illuminate the area. I keep my eyes peeled for any sign from beyond, but don't see anything other than trees on our walk.

We find Val waiting outside the tape, pacing nervously. George paces with her. "Rylan," she calls when she sees me.

I hurry to her side and give her a hug. "You doing okay?"

"I guess. What a night."

I look toward the crime scene. Ford and Tyler are standing on the far side of the tree, staring and discussing. The tree is wide, but I see yellow ropes wrapped around it again.

"Is this like Celeste? Is the body tied to a tree again?"

"Another young girl." Val's voice breaks. "I think I know her."

"Oh, Val. How awful. Who is it?" Mickey asks.

"I don't actually know her, but I've seen her at the donut shop. She's a friend of the other girl. I think her name is Marie."

Mickey puts her hand to her mouth. "Two friends murdered? How terrible."

"What are the odds?" I ask, my mind racing. "Did you tell Ford?"

"I did. He said he knew her, too. They interviewed her about Celeste."

I want to ask questions, but don't want to upset Val. Instead, I make my way slowly along the yellow tape, trying not to draw attention to myself. If Ford or Tyler spots me, they'll surely send me away.

Once I'm far enough around the tree, I can see her. She's tied like Celeste, but the similarities end there.

Val is suddenly with me. "Don't look. It's bad."

Too late. I've already seen the blood. Lots of blood. Dripping down her cut jeans, leaking from gashes on her arms. The smell of it heavy despite the crisp night air.

The neck is the worst, a massive gaping wound.

I turn away, disgusted. The remains of my dinner flip sickeningly in my stomach. I swallow hard and breathe through my nose to keep it down.

Mickey is about to look, but I grab her by the shoulder and turn her around. "Don't. Trust me, don't."

She looks at my face and sees something that makes her

agree not to look. We walk back around the tree where we can't see what is left of Marie.

We stand in the shadows thrown by the moon, rubbing our arms against the misty night chill.

"Who the hell would do that to her?" I say, breaking the silence.

"Someone sick," Val says.

I wipe my face and feel something sticky. When I pull my fingers away, they are stained with something dark in the moonlight.

"What...?" I look down and see blood on my shirt. "How did I get blood on me?"

Val has on a dark shirt, but I catch a gleam of wetness on it. "Do you have blood on you?"

Val looks at her shirt, pulling it out. "I don't know."

Mickey steps closer with her phone flashlight on. "That looks like blood."

Val pulls the sweater over her head and tosses it on the ground. "Oh, m-my God. How did that get there?" She stands in only a tank top, searching it for blood, too.

"Rylan, is that you?" Ford suddenly says behind me. He must have been drawn by Mickey's light. She shines it on his face, then abruptly turns it off.

"Hey, Ford." I try to be casual. "Val called to tell me what happened."

Ford studies Val, sees the sweater on the ground and her in only a tank top against the spring chill. He raises an eyebrow in question.

"She, um, she got hot," I say. I don't want to tell him about the blood.

He reaches to my face and runs a finger across my cheek, leaving a line of heat behind.

"And this?" he pulls his finger away and it is stained dark.

"Mud?" I try.

"Stop messing around, Rylan. What is going on?" He bends to pick up the sweater, sniffs the stain.

"Blood. Lots of blood." He looks to Val who has grown pale. "Want to tell me how you got so much blood on your shirt?" He flips his gaze to me. "And why it is on your face?"

I wipe my hand on my jeans surreptitiously.

"I don't know. I did give her a hug. I must have gotten it on me then."

He turns his full attention to Val. "I was going to take your statement later, but maybe you should tell me now how exactly you found Marie way out here in the middle of the night."

"It was George. He found her."

Ford looks at George, who has been lying down this whole time. "The dog again? Is that like how he found Celeste?"

Val looks at me for support. "I already told him how I found her. It's okay. Just tell us what happened tonight."

"I was in bed when George started barking. He was really carrying on, so I got up to see what was happening. He scratched at the door and wanted out. When I opened the door, he bolted into the woods. So I tossed on that sweater and my boots and followed to get him to come home."

"Do you make it a habit to follow your dog out at night?" Ford asks.

"No, I don't. But he was really going nuts, and after what happened here the other night, I've been on edge. I thought maybe someone was out there wanting to get a look at the crime scene or something. I had the idea of chasing them away."

"But you didn't call the police?"

"All I knew was George heard something. What was I supposed to tell the police?"

"Did you hear something once you got into the woods?"

"I didn't hear anything. I called George several times and he finally came back. He was agitated and kept running back this direction. I got curious, and frankly a little scared. I followed him to this," she points to the tree. "At first, I didn't realize she was here. Like I said, I thought some sicko was coming to look at the crime scene. I had no idea there would be a second body on the tree."

"What did you do after you found her?"

"I called 911 of course."

Ford looks at each of us in turn. "Then how did you get blood on you? Did you touch the body?"

"Of course not. I don't know how the blood got there."

He nods, thinking. Then looks at me in apology. "You know this doesn't look good, Val. Two dead on your property, you covered with blood."

Val takes a step back. "What are you saying? Y-you don't think I had anything to do with this."

"Too soon to tell. I certainly hope you're not the type of person that would mutilate a young woman like what happened here."

"Holy flip, you can't be serious," I practically shout. "You know she didn't do this."

"I only know what the clues tell us. Right now, she's covered with physical evidence."

"She's not covered. She just has a stain on her shirt," I counter. "If she'd done this, she would be covered in blood."

"She could have cleaned up before she called us. It's happened before."

Mickey has been watching the whole thing, quietly listening, petting George to keep him still. Hearing our agitation, George stands and whines. "Shh," she soothes.

"I did not do this," Val says.

"What the—" Mickey says, staring at her hand. It is stained dark red.

Ford looks at her hand and then at George. He reaches to pet the black dog. His hand comes away red, too."

"See," I push. "George must have gotten the blood on him and he got it on Val's shirt."

Ford looks at me. "You know I can't let it go at that. I have to follow the evidence."

"That is the evidence," I point at his red hand. "You have her blood on you now. Maybe you did it."

"Don't be absurd, Rylan."

"You're the one being absurd."

"What is all the racket over here?" Tyler joins our group. "Marrero is having a fit."

"Ford thinks Val is a suspect," I say.

Tyler looks at Ford, then at Val.

"She has Marie's blood on her and this is her property. Do you have anyone that can vouch for where you've been tonight?" Ford asks.

"You know I live alone," Val says, her voice sinking.

Tyler seems reluctant. "We'll have to search your house to be sure."

"Search anything you want. I did not do this."

"We'll have to detain you while we do the search," Ford says.

I want to pound on him in anger. I clench my fists instead. "Seriously? Ford, why are you doing this?"

"I'm just doing my job."

"Since when was it your job to harass innocent women because their dog got them dirty?"

"Since someone is killing young women on her property. Until we solve this, everyone is a suspect." He steps closer, and looms over me. "Now stay out of it before I haul you in for obstruction."

"You wouldn't dare." Almost arrested twice in one night. That's a record, even for me.

"Maybe I'll just let Frazier finish what he started with the trespassing."

I'd wondered if Frazier would tell him with all that was going on tonight. Apparently so.

"That's different." I raise my chin in defiance.

"Don't push me." He steps closer, so close I can see the fine lines at the corners of his eyes.

Tyler steps between us. "Okay, Rylan, that's enough. If you promise to be good, we won't take you in." My chest is heaving in anger, but I step away from Ford.

"Ms. Flynn, unfortunately we need to detain you," Tyler continues.

"That's not fair." Mickey joins the fight.

"Don't you start, too," Tyler says. "We have plenty of cuffs and cars to haul you all in."

Mickey looks at the ground.

"It's okay, girls," Val says, putting her hands together in front of her. "They won't find anything because I didn't do anything. Go ahead and cuff me. You're going to feel silly when you find nothing and have to let me go."

"We don't need to do that. We will just put you in a car for now. As long as you don't resist," Ford says.

"How gallant of you," I snap.

"Your last warning, Rylan," he replies, guiding Val by the shoulder. He says to Tyler, "I'll take her to a car. Have the techs bag that sweater."

Ford leads Val away and I watch helplessly. "Don't worry," I say. "I'll call Keaton and he'll take care of this."

When Val is gone, Mickey steps closer. "What do we do now?"

"They won't find anything. I guess we wait," I say.

"What you do is go home," Tyler says.

George pushes his nose against my leg. "What about George? Can we take him with us?"

"He has evidence on him. He has to stay with us."

"Can't you just take a sample from his fur or something?"

Tyler gives in a little. "I suppose we can do that." He calls to a tech who comes to take the dog's sample and the sweater. We all stand silently as the tech does her job.

"There, you happy?" Tyler asks.

"So can we take him now?"

"Take him. And don't come back to this scene. I heard what you two were up to last night. Don't do it again," he warns.

"I know, I know. Or you'll arrest us, right?"

Tyler suddenly laughs out loud. "I see why Ford always looks so worn out when he deals with you. Now, go home."

I tell George to follow and Mickey and I hurry away. I don't know if I should be insulted by what he said about Ford or happy I make an impression on him. Right now I'm so angry with him I'm just glad he's upset with me, too.

I drop a yawning Mickey at her house and then drive home with George in the backseat. I'd rubbed most of the blood off with some handfuls of leaves, but I'm sure he's getting more on the upholstery.

There was no way I was leaving him behind after I made such a fuss about it. If he gets blood on the car, I'll deal with it tomorrow.

It's not until he bounds out of the backseat and runs across the small front yard that I think maybe this wasn't a good idea. My house barely holds me, let alone a large dog. I'll just have to make the best of it.

I let George do his business on one of my bushes and then open my front door. He rushes to go inside, but stops and backs away with a whine.

I try to urge him to go in, but he looks at me as if to say, "Are you kidding?"

"Rylan, you're finally home," I hear Mom say from her room, and George's reluctance makes sense.

"She won't hurt you," I tell him. I can't leave him outside, so I tug on his collar until he is far enough in that I can shut the door. He cowers on the mat, his tail tucked. I didn't even think about Mom and what her presence would do to a dog. Let alone the other spirits that like to visit when I sleep.

"It's okay," I soothe and he licks my hand. "We need to get you cleaned up, then we'll go to bed."

This time when I start down the crowded path toward the bathroom, he follows.

I duck my head into Mom's room and tell her goodnight. She sees George.

"Is that your aunt's dog? What's he doing here?"

I have no desire to tell her about the murders and Val being in custody, so I just say I'm babysitting for fun.

Mom believes me and starts to brush her hair like she often does. "Okay, dear. Good night, then."

George is less than pleased to be taking a bath in the middle of the night, but I don't want blood stains on my bed. I manage to get his front paws into the tub, but have to lift his rear to get him all in. He knocks my many shampoo bottles off the ledge, which startles him further.

I do my best to keep him calm and rinse him with the hand-held shower wand. Bright red streaks run down the white porcelain. I have to look away from the blood, have to block out where it came from.

Having a murder victim's blood running down my drain feels all kinds of wrong. It makes me shiver a little.

I pretend it's just ketchup and finish washing the dog. After his first few moments of upset, George settles down and resigns to being washed.

With lots of "good dogs" and the promise of treats I don't have, I manage to rinse him until the water runs clear.

Then he shakes and I'm drenched in wet dog hair.

I quickly towel him off as he shakes and wriggles. He breaks away from me and bolts into the hall, rubbing his face on the carpet, rolling on his back. His antics make me laugh. Despite everything that has happened, I'm glad to have him with me tonight.

He follows me to the kitchen, carefully moving down the paths like he's used to being in such a crowded house.

Searching the fridge, I find some lunchmeat. I pull out a slice and throw it to George. He catches it mid-air and takes it down in one gulp. "Was that good?" I toss him another. Only then do I realize how hungry I am. Dinner was hours and hours ago. I should be asleep. I take a slice of the ham and roll it around a pickle. The snack will have to do for now.

I suddenly yawn around a half-chewed bite. "Time for bed. You'll have to sleep with me."

George wriggles his butt and follows me to my room. I put an old blanket on top of the many blankets and pillows already stacked on the mattress. George climbs onto the blanket, twirls around and settles down.

Only then, do I remember he's wet. But I don't care. I curl onto an open corner of the bed, pull some covers over me and close my eyes. I hold the cross charm on my bracelet, and say a prayer for Val.

I hope with the dog here, the terror in Keaton's room will be quiet.

SEVENTEEN

KEATON FLYNN

The phone rings, waking me up. Sheryl, my fiancé, stirs next to me. "This better be important. It's the middle of the night," she grumbles.

I check the caller ID and see Aunt Val's name. I sit upright, fully awake. This can't be good.

"Is everything okay?" I ask without saying hello. Images of Dad in the hospital fill my mind.

"No. Everything is not okay."

"Is it Dad? Or Rylan?" I can only imagine my sister getting into trouble this late at night.

"Nothing like that. They are fine. I'm in trouble."

Sheryl sits up with a worried look. "What is it?" she mouths silently, pushing her hair out of her face.

I cover the phone and tell her, "It's Aunt Val." I uncover the phone. "What kind of trouble?" I check the time. I can't imagine Val even up at this time of night, let alone in trouble.

"Will you come?"

"Of course, but come where? Val, what's going on?" I start pacing the room.

"You know that girl Celeste that we found dead here?"

"I do." The whole town knows about it, but I don't point that out.

"There's been another one. Another murder." Her voice breaks and she hiccups a little. "It was a-awful. So much b-blood."

"They don't think you had anything to do with it, do they? That's not what you mean."

"That's exactly what I mean." Her voice turns hard. "That Ford Pierce is taking me in for questioning. George found the girl and he got her blood on him which got it on me. They think that looks suspicious."

Sheryl is watching me intently, trying to gauge the conversation by my responses.

"That's ridiculous. He should know better."

"That's what Rylan said."

"Why was Rylan there?"

"Because I called her."

"You called her to a crime scene?"

"I didn't know who else to call. I was hoping she could see the girl's ghost and get some information out of her."

That's actually a good plan. "And did she?"

"No. At least, not yet."

"Where are you now?"

"I've been detained and put in a car to wait. They are going to search my house for evidence. They can do that right?"

"Did you give your consent?"

Val is quiet a moment. "I'm not sure. It all happened so fast. I think I said something like search away you won't find anything."

"That sounds like consent. They will probably ask again just to be sure they have all their Is dotted."

"Should I give it?"

"If you have nothing to hide, then it wouldn't hurt."

"I didn't think I had anything to hide before, but they found that blood on my sweater and ran crazy with it."

I scan my room for some pants to pull on. "Just sit tight, and I'll be right there."

"Where am I going to go?"

"Good point. Just hang in there and give me a few minutes."

"I'll be here," she says ruefully. "Thank you, Keaton. Truly."

I hang up and meet Sheryl's questioning look. "There's been another murder on Aunt Val's property. I really shouldn't say more than that at this time."

"Always the lawyer," she grumbles. "Is your aunt okay?"

I'm not sure how to answer. "I can't. I really can't. I'm her representation."

She sits up, all interest. "Why would she need representation? Did she do something?"

"Of course not. Now, please stop asking questions," I say and kiss her forehead.

"I know, no questions. I just can't help myself."

"Do I wear dress clothes or should I wear jeans?"

Sheryl takes the question seriously, which is part of why I love her. She is always ready to help. "Depends. Are you going to the woods or to the police station?" She scrunches her face. "How about khakis? That should be dressy but casual."

I suddenly wonder why I'm worried about my pants. I grow sober. "It sounds bad." I say, mentally bracing for being on scene at a murder. "She said there was a lot of blood."

Sheryl climbs out of bed and puts her arms around my shoulders. "It will be okay. You have been on scenes before."

I take a deep breath and take in the scent of her shampoo. "You're right. I'll be okay. I just need to worry about Val."

"And your sister," she says ruefully. Sheryl and Rylan have never really gotten along. Sheryl is a nurse and deals with the here and now of things. She's never come out and said the words, but I get the feeling she thinks Rylan is faking her abilities.

"Yes, my sister is there. Looks like it will be a long night."

It's easy to find the crime scene. The lights reflect on the sky from a mile away. I slow to a crawl and an officer directs me to keep driving. I pull over and roll my window down.

Officer Frazier steps to the car. "You need to keep moving. No sightseers tonight, please." He doesn't even look at me.

"It's me, Keaton Flynn," I say. "I'm here to see my client."

"Sorry, Keaton, I didn't recognize you. Your sister get herself arrested or something?"

"It's not my sister, and I can't talk about it right now."

Frazier looks confused for a moment, but lets me park behind a cruiser. I want to ask which car Val is in, but he probably won't know.

I search the cars on the side of the road, until I see her waving from the backseat of a cruiser. Seeing my beloved aunt like that makes my chest burn with anger. Ford may be my best friend and head detective, but this is ridiculous.

I open Val's door and peer inside. She looks like she's been crying. "You okay in there?"

"I suppose," she says, bravely. "How long will they keep me in here?"

"As long as it takes. I'll do what I can to speed them along. We know you're innocent. This is just a misunderstanding." I scan the woods, the lights in the distance, between the trees. "I'll go see what I can find out."

I gently close the car door and start into the woods. My feet slow as I grow closer to the tree surrounded by all the commotion. I really don't want to see a dead girl tonight.

From here, I can see her head hanging to the side, can see the glow of red in the floodlights.

I skirt the scene, approaching from behind the tree. I stop at the yellow tape and watch. Coroner Marrero is leaning close to the body, inspecting her mouth.

"Just like I figured," he says. He sticks tweezers into the mouth and pulls something shiny out. "Another coin." He drops the coin into a plastic evidence bag and seals it. He then notices me. "I didn't know the DA sent someone already," he says. His eyes skim over my khakis and I suddenly wish I was wearing a suit.

"I'm not here on behalf of the DA's office."

"You here for Val?" Ford asks, stepping around the tree.

"She called. She's pretty scared."

"I can imagine," he says enigmatically. "Sorry about that."

"Do you need to keep her in that car? You know she didn't do this." I motion to the tree, but won't look in that direction.

"I know this sucks for her, but she had the victim's blood on her clothes. What else can I do?"

"Do you know it was the victim's? Maybe she cut herself. Did you run a test on it?"

Ford cocks his head. "Is that how we're playing this?"

"I'm just doing what's best for my client."

"Client? If she's so innocent, why does she need a lawyer already?"

"Just playing it smart."

"Since when did you start working for the defense?"

"Since you cuffed my aunt and stuffed her in a cruiser."

"We didn't cuff her."

"How kind of you." This conversation is getting away from me. Ford is my friend and we usually get along well, even when we don't see eye to eye on a case. Seeing Aunt Val's red-rimmed eyes and panicked expression has got my protective instincts up.

Ford studies me. He's three inches taller and has to look down a bit. Ever since ninth grade, when he had a growth spurt and surpassed me, I've resented those three inches.

I straighten my back and shoulders. "She said you were holding her until you could search her house. Can you at least release her into my custody while you do that? Looks like you will be here for a while. It's not fair to keep her captive up there in that car all night."

"Captive?" He raises his eyebrows. "What do you think your boss will say when he finds out you're working for the other side?"

"He'll understand I will do what I need for my family."

Ford finally shakes his head. "Go take her. Just don't let her anywhere near that house until we finish with it."

"I'll do that."

"And make sure your sister has taken that dog she fought for."

"Rylan has George?"

"She and Mickey took him a while ago. Wouldn't let us hold him at animal control."

"I'll make sure," I call over my shoulder as I trudge back to the road. I'm anxious to go get Val and leave before Ford changes his mind.

Val practically falls out of the car when I open the door.

"You made them see they were wrong? I can go home?"

"No, I just got Ford to let you come with me. You're still a suspect until they clear you officially."

"How long will that take?"

"I don't know. I'm sorry. I will do my best to get them to expedite the search of your house. Hopefully, then they will let you go, based on lack of evidence."

"It's that bad?"

"Maybe."

"But you work for the DA. That has to mean something."

"Right now I work for you."

She looks at me, her face full of appreciation. "Thank you."

"Now don't go getting all mushy on me. It's the least I can do." She puts her arm around my waist and I lead her to my car.

"Wait, what about George?"

"Ford said Rylan took him."

"Bless that girl," she says, her arm slipping from my waist. "She's the best."

I take on a whole criminal case and Rylan just babysits a dog, and she still wins.

EIGHTEEN

FORD PIERCE

The Flynn family has made this already-horrific murder scene even more complicated. After Rylan leaves with the dog, and Keaton leaves with our suspect, I can finally focus where I need to. On the victim.

Ashby is a small town, and I've often seen the bodies of people I know. Those are usually accidents or natural causes. I've seen some horrific things, but this—this is way worse.

Made even more so since we just talked to Marie Prestwood. That can't be a coincidence. My mind races, looking for a connection that makes sense. A reason two girls that knew each other would end up tied to this same tree.

What the killer did to Marie is far and above what happened to Celeste. The details are the same. The coin in the mouth, the cuts to the body. Marie is even wearing the same necklace with the horse charm that Celeste had on.

I've never seen so much blood as I do with this scene. I can easily see how George would be attracted to it, would carry it in his fur and get it on Valerie Flynn.

Still, I don't believe in coincidences. As hard as it is to believe Val would murder two young women and then call the cops on herself, I find it harder to swallow that they are both on her property. It is common for killers to be the ones to find the bodies. They love being part of the investigation, being close to the havoc they've caused.

Is Val Flynn really capable of doing such a horrible thing? The aunt Keaton and I spent weeks with in the summer as kids? The same woman who makes donuts for the whole town each morning?

You never know what someone is capable of. As much as I hate to admit it, it's not impossible that she did this.

Marrero suddenly motions for Tyler and me to join him.

"I found something that might be useful," he says, pointing to the cuts on Marie's arms. "The cuts here are quite distinctive."

We both look at the man with interest. "How do you mean?" Tyler asks.

"In my opinion, it looks like these were caused by a serrated knife."

"Like a steak knife?" I ask.

"Exactly."

"Like you'd find in a kitchen," I muse.

"You ready to check out the house?" Tyler asks. "Maybe there's a knife missing from the knife block."

"Definitely."

I follow him through the woods toward the cabin tucked among the trees. I visited here with Keaton a few times growing up and have long admired the place. The A-frame house with wood siding fits right into the landscape. The porch stretches the length of the front.

I take the three steps up onto the porch, my flashlight checking out every step, every board.

"Look," I say pointing to a dark streak on the top step. "Think that's more blood?"

Tyler shines his flashlight on the stain. "Could be." He

checks further along the porch, and finds another dark streak. The door to the house is white and has several more streaks on it. Even the door handle has blood on it.

"If she was trying to hide the evidence, she didn't do a very good job of it," Tyler says.

My stomach sinks. I still can't wrap my head around Val being our killer. "Or it could be from the dog, like they said."

"But if the dog led her to the body, I can see blood being on her sweater. The problem is, if she called from the scene and didn't come back here like she claims, then how did this blood get here?"

A good point. "Unless she's lying."

"Either way, it doesn't look good. Let's see what's inside."

We let ourselves into the unlocked front door. The light is on. We look around carefully. I'm hoping we don't find anything.

Tyler looks in the kitchen sink. "Bingo," he says excitedly.

"What is it?" I hurry to his side and look in the sink. There are drops of blood on the rim and a residue of it near the drain. At the bottom of the sink is a steak knife covered in blood.

"Think it came from here?" Tyler asks, pointing to the knife block, which is missing a knife.

"I really hoped she didn't do this," I say, my heart sinking to my toes. "Not Val Flynn."

Tyler calls down to the crime scene. "We need techs up here at the house. We found the knife."

My heart sinks further when I realize that I let a brutal killer go with Keaton.

I scramble for my phone and pull up his number. "You ready to clear my aunt?" he asks.

"Actually, I need you to hold her until I can get a unit to your house."

"You have to be kidding."

"I'm not kidding. We found more evidence. It looks like your aunt isn't the kind of woman we always thought she was."

"You know you've got this all wrong. Val would never do that."

"I hoped I was wrong, but it's right here in front of me."

Keaton sighs heavily. "I'll have her at the station in a little while. You don't need to send a unit for her."

After I hang up with Keaton, I continue searching the house. I expect to find something relating to the occult like we did at Celeste's apartment, but we don't. We don't find anything else incriminating; the knife is enough. Techs come to take it for comparison, process the house, and take samples of the blood stains. I'm certain they will come back as Marie's blood.

Once we finish up at the house, Tyler and I drive back to the station to talk to Val. As promised, she and Keaton are waiting in the lobby for us. Val looks terrified, Keaton looks angry.

"We came as promised," he says.

"I appreciate it." I look at Val, trying to reconcile the bloody scene with the middle-aged, mild-mannered woman before me. She's wearing a Purdue University sweatshirt she must have borrowed from Keaton. There's not a trace of blood on it.

"Are you going to arrest me?" Her voice is meek.

"Let's just get settled in a room first," I say as gently as possible. I hate doing this. Then I think of Celeste and Marie and my resolve hardens.

Once we are all in the interrogation room and seated, Keaton asks, "So what did you supposedly find in her house?"

"We'll ask the questions," Tyler says.

"My client isn't talking."

"I didn't do anything!" Val exclaims. "I would never hurt those girls. I knew them from when they'd visit The Hole and come in for donuts, but I didn't have anything against them."

Keaton tries to quiet her, but she brushes him off. "Whatever you found at my house, I didn't do it."

"What did you find?" Keaton asks.

"Blood stains on the porch and in the sink for one," I say.

"You said you found Marie then called 911 and waited for the police to arrive. If you didn't go back to your house, how did blood get there?" Tyler asks.

Val sits back as if she's been punched. "I don't know. There must be a mistake," she whispers.

I look her over. She seems to be telling the truth, but I can't fall for that.

"We found the knife," I say.

"What knife?"

"The knife used to cut Marie. It was in your sink."

Val goes limp and pale. "That's not possible."

"We're done here," Keaton says. "You have no way of knowing if the blood you supposedly found belongs to the victim. At least not until the DNA comes back, and that will take a while. And that knife could just be a coincidence." His voice shakes and he doesn't seem to believe his own words.

"Presumptive test shows it's human blood. Want to explain that?" Tyler says.

Val opens her mouth, but nothing comes out.

"Don't answer that," Keaton says at the same time. "As I said, we are done here." Keaton pushes his chair back.

"You can't take her," I say. "We're holding her until we get the DNA back."

Val makes a strangled sound. "Don't worry, Aunt Val," Keaton says. "They can only keep you for forty-eight hours at the most. We'll have you out before that." He tries to sound upbeat, but even I hear the worry in his voice. He watches helplessly as Tyler places cuffs on Val and we lead her out of the room.

She looks over her shoulder at her nephew. "I'll do everything I can," he calls down the hall.

Never would I have thought she'd butcher two young women.

I hope the DNA comes back as Val's blood. I hope there's an innocent explanation for all of this.

Mostly, I worry that if we have the wrong person in custody, the real killer is out there still.

NINETEEN

RYLAN FLYNN

I've barely slept when Keaton calls.

I uncurl myself from the blanket and answer the phone. "I take it Val called you." I yawn. "I'm glad. I hated to leave her, but they made me go."

"Listen, Rylan, its bad."

I sit up in bed and turn on the light. George lifts his head, curious.

"What happened?"

"They took her. They said they found a bloody knife at her house so they took her in. They're holding her."

"She's in jail? That can't be right. Isn't there anything you can do?"

"I can try, but they are within their rights if they have evidence against her."

"There can't be evidence. She didn't do this."

"I know that, but there is blood and the murder weapon in her house. The blood on her sweater, I could talk away, but she never went back to the house. How did it all get there?"

I fiddle with the charms on my bracelet, nervously thinking. "There has to be a mistake."

"I'll keep you posted, but, at this point, we're basically waiting on the DNA results."

"Thanks for telling me." I climb over George and out of bed. "Have you told Dad yet?"

"No. I didn't want to wake him and get him all worried. There's nothing he can do."

A plan is starting to form in my head. "There's something I can do, though. Look, I've got to let you go. Call me if anything changes."

My mind has already moved on. The best way to save Val is to find the true killer. If Celeste's ghost was unable to talk to me, maybe Marie's will.

I didn't see her at the crime scene, which seems like the most logical place to look for her. I can't go back now; the police are crawling all over and I certainly wouldn't be welcome.

Instead, I go out on my back patio and look at the full moon. Where would Marie's ghost go if she is out there?

"Marie? If you can hear this, come find me. I know you have something to tell me."

I listen to the night wind and search the shadows of my backyard. A tingle starts on my shoulders and wriggles down my back. I look harder, focus on the various shapes of bushes and trees.

I'm not sure this will work. I've never tried to summon a ghost to my house before. They normally come uninvited.

I call out to Marie again and listen and wait. After several moments, a shadow begins to form next to a tree. I can't make out the shape, but the tingle in my shoulders grows more intense.

Something or someone is there.

"Come on out. I won't hurt you," I coax.

The shadow solidifies and takes the shape of a young woman.

It's Marie.

In the moonlight, I see her. She looks just like she did on the tree. It is hard to look at all the blood stains and the rips in her clothing. I especially don't want to look at the slit in her throat. She steps onto my patio, a terrifying figure.

"Marie. It's okay. I won't hurt you."

She tilts her head, listening, holding her neck.

"I know you're scared," I continue. "I need your help."

She tries to talk but a hissing sound comes out. Her slit throat makes it impossible to form the words.

She suddenly coughs, and a coin similar to the one Celeste had falls out of her mouth. She bends to pick it up, holds it in the light. Her face pinches in anger as she looks at it. I notice the triangle on one side and the upside-down triangle on the other. Similar to the other coin, but without the extra lines.

"Do you know what the coin is?" I ask Marie.

She nods, still staring at it, turning it over in her hand.

"Do you know why it is in your mouth?"

She nods again.

"Do you know the man that put it there?"

Her face scrunches in confusion and she shakes her head, then nods it. Not a straight answer.

"Who did this?" I motion to her neck.

She opens her mouth to speak, but the same hissing sound as before comes out. She touches her neck, gingerly running a finger across the deep bloody slice that nearly decapitated her. Pain clouds her expression.

"Who did this to you?" I press.

The window to Keaton's room is behind me and something begins pounding on the glass.

Startled, Marie turns at the sound, poised to flee.

"Don't go," I beg. "Tell me who did this."

She looks at the window that is now shaking from the pounding, then she looks back.

She tosses the coin in my direction. I try to catch it, but it disappears as soon as she does.

Once she is gone, the pounding stops. My heart beats furiously and I gasp to catch my breath.

So close. I was so close to learning the truth.

The next day, I wake with one thought. I have to set Val free. I try to call her at the jail, but they won't let me talk to her. I call Keaton, but he doesn't have any more news.

All I can think about is how terrified Val must be. She's never even gotten a parking ticket. I can't imagine what she's feeling.

I run my entire encounter with Marie over in my head, searching for a clue in the little that I was able to get from her. Celeste didn't know the man that killed her and Marie said yes and no. What does that mean?

Ford needs to know what I learned. Maybe something will help him in the investigation. He's on my list of least favorite people right now, but I don't care. I will work with him if it will help Val.

After taking George out on the back patio, I place the call.

"I figured you weren't talking to me," Ford says when I get him on the phone.

"Honestly, I don't want to after the stunt you pulled last night."

His voice hardens. "It isn't a stunt. We have clear evidence that links your aunt to the murder."

"And I have evidence from the victim." George sniffs around the place Marie stood last night.

"You talked to her?"

"Well, not exactly. She has her throat cut, so she couldn't talk. I did find out she has another coin in her mouth. This one is a little different, with triangles on it again but not the extra bars."

"We found that at the scene last night. Similar to the first coin, just a slightly different symbol. What else did you learn?"

"That she knows what the coin is and why it is in her mouth, but she doesn't know the man that put it there."

"Because Val is not a man."

"Val didn't do this."

"I'm just following the evidence," he says.

"Your evidence is flawed," I counter.

"Your evidence is from a ghost."

"I'd trust a ghost more than I'd trust you right now," I snap.

"Are we going to argue again? I really don't have time for that."

"Neither do I. I have a murder to solve."

"Don't even think about it. You stay far away from this case."

"Or what? You can't stop me from snooping around as long as I'm not breaking any laws."

He sighs heavily. "I'm asking as your friend *and* as a detective. Please, just stay out of it. We already have a suspect."

"You keep on punishing an innocent woman, while I catch the real killer." With that, I hang up on him, my heart racing. Why does Ford get me so angry so easily?

More importantly, what am I getting myself into?

Despite my bravado with Ford, I have no idea how to catch a killer. I only know Val needs someone on her side, and that someone is me.

I let George back into the house and he wriggles through the kitchen path. I put down a bowl of water for him and look for something to give him for breakfast. My kitchen is packed with stuff, but little of it is edible. I find a box of Pop-Tarts and open the crinkly wrapper. I hand one to George who wolfs it down in two bites, then I nibble on the other one for my breakfast.

I'll have to get him something healthier than a Pop-Tart if he's going to be staying with me for a while. Deciding to make a trip to the store, I settle him in the bathroom before I leave. I don't want him roaming the house and knocking a stack of stuff over on himself.

"Sorry about this," I say, rubbing his wide head. "Just gonna make a quick run to the grocery store and I'll be right back with some real food."

I hate to waste time on a grocery run when a killer is on the loose, but the dog's got to eat.

While I'm at the store, I add a few essentials to my cart before I enter the dog-food aisle. The number of choices is unsettling. As I'm studying a bag with a black lab that looks like George on it, I hear the last voice I expected.

"Rylan Flynn, in the flesh. Searching for ghosts in the dog-food aisle?" Lindy Parker asks.

I freeze with my back to her. I am not in the mood for her today. After plastering a fake smile on my face, I slowly turn.

"Lindy," I say tightly. "Good to see you," I lie.

She looks in my cart at the eggs and milk and the Little Debbie brownies. I don't miss the look of disgust on her face. She's probably never eaten a Little Debbie brownie in her life.

Her loss.

She runs her hand over her long red curls with a smirk. I self-consciously touch my hair, then remember I'd skinned it back into a tight ponytail. I don't even have any makeup on. Lindy's makeup is nearly flawless. Nearly. She has a small smudge from her mascara in the corner of one eye. I focus on the imperfection as I talk.

"Can I help you with something?" I ask, as I heft the dog-food bag into my cart. It lands with a rattle. Lindy's cart only has a tiny bag of designer dog food.

"I just wanted to say how sorry I am about your recent—" she pauses and lowers her voice. "—family troubles."

I'm taken aback that she knows about Val. "If you mean about how the police have unfairly taken my aunt into custody, then I appreciate your condolences."

"I'd think Ford Pierce would take it a little easier on you guys with your history and all."

Holy flip, does she know I have a crush on Ford? Does the whole town know?

"What do you mean history?"

"Him and Keaton being friends for so long." Her smile leads me to believe there's more to it. Either she knows about my feelings or she's just messing with my head. Knowing Lindy, she just wants to get me riled up.

I don't take the bait.

"Ford is just doing his job."

Why am I defending him?

She smiles enigmatically. "Of course, *you'd* say that." I don't want to look too closely at that comment.

I push my cart past her. "I need to go. As you said, my family is in a bit of trouble and I have work to do."

She grips my arm as I pass and leans close. "I'm watching you, Rylan Flynn. If I find out you did anything to those girls to boost your ratings, I'll make sure your 'friend' locks you up."

I'm shaken by the direct accusation. Lindy Parker has always been a pain, but she's never seemed so unhinged as she does now. "You need help if you think that's what's going on here."

"What is going on then?"

I pull my arm from her grip. "A psycho is killing young women in some kind of ritual. My aunt has been framed. That's what's going on."

"What kind of ritual?" she asks, flipping back to that saccharine-sweet voice she uses on her show.

"How would I know? Something sick."

"Isn't that your forte, freaky rituals with you and your dad? From what I hear, now you have your brother wrapped up in this mess, too."

She seems honestly concerned about Keaton. I know she has worked with him at the DA's office, but her concern seems more personal.

"Keaton can handle himself, and, besides, I thought you were an expert on what I do. The ghosts come to me, Lindy. I don't do rituals to call them in." I think about last night and how I did call Marie. I didn't do any ritual, though.

"I have other things to do than study you."

I push my cart down the aisle, away from this crazy conversation. "I have other things to do, too." I pause at the corner, and say over my shoulder, "Always nice to chat, Lindy." I use the most sarcastic voice I can. If my mother was still alive, she'd be disappointed at my manners.

TWENTY

RYLAN FLYNN

I spend the rest of the morning on the internet researching the symbols on the coin. The first coin had the Wiccan symbols for air and earth. The second coin had the symbols for fire and water. That much I figured out, but beyond that I couldn't find anything to help with the investigation. I debate calling Ford to tell him about the symbols, but decide against it. He has the whole police department at his disposal. I'm sure they can find out more than I did on a Google search.

I sit back on my bed and pet George. I'm no closer to finding the truth than I was an hour ago.

"I gotta do something to help your momma," I tell the dog.

He licks my hand in response. Although I know it's my imagination, his brown eyes seem to bore into mine, begging me for help.

I gently push his head away. "Stop looking at me like that. I'm doing what I can."

He puts his muzzle on my knee and humphs.

"I know," I tell him. "I need to do something else." I shut the computer and place it on top of a pile of stuffed animals. I wait a moment to make sure it doesn't slide into the abyss of stuff in my room, then climb across the pillows and blankets. I'm slightly out of breath when I reach my bedroom door.

It hits me that the murdered girls knew each other and they both knew Kimmie Steele. I pull on my black Chuck Taylor sneakers and head to The Hole. Kimmie might be working. I have a few questions to ask her.

The Hole is busy with the after-church crowd. I feel a bit guilty that I didn't go to watch Dad's sermon this morning, but I'm sure he will forgive me. "God doesn't only live in church," he's said many times. "But he likes it when you come visit."

I make a mental promise to go next week, and head inside the donut shop.

The familiar smell of baked yeast and sugar fills my nose, and for a moment I worry Val will never return to her beloved shop. I push that thought away and get in line to order.

Kimmie is behind the counter. Her smile looks tight and she has dark smudges under her eyes. I'm not surprised. She just lost two friends to a horrific crime and her boss has been taken in as a suspect. If anything, I'm surprised she's at work today.

When I reach my turn in line, Kimmie's face grows even tighter, her forced smile faltering.

"Rylan, good to see you," she says. "Sorry about Val. I know she didn't do it."

"I'm surprised you're here after everything that's happened to your friends."

Kimmie looks away, and then back again. "I didn't have much choice. Eileen opened the shop this morning and made the donuts, but Val normally runs the counter. Your brother called and asked me if I would come in and help out."

"We really appreciate it. Val would hate to be closed on a Sunday."

Kimmie gives a half-hearted shrug. "I can use the money, anyways. I might not have a job much longer if Val goes to jail." Her voice is unusually devoid of emotion.

"Val will be out and back to work soon. Don't you worry."

Kimmie eyes the line behind me. "What can I get for you?"

"Actually, I wanted to talk to you. If I wait until you're not so busy, can we chat?"

Her eyes narrow suspiciously. "Chat about what? I've already talked to the police. Why would I talk to you too?"

She has me there. "As a favor to Val," I try.

Kimmie chews her lower lip a moment, thinking. "Okay. Just a few questions. I don't have anything to hide. Just wait until the rush is over." She forces a smile and slips back into work mode. "Now, would you like a donut?"

All I've eaten today is the Pop-Tart I shared with George, and my stomach really wants a donut. "I'll take a bear claw."

She serves me the pastry and says, "On the house. Val wouldn't like me charging her family."

I say thank you and take my bear claw to a corner table. I watch the crowded room fill up and then clear out after a while. Once the line is served, Kimmie joins me.

She slides into the seat opposite mine.

"What do you want to ask me? I already told the police that I didn't know Marie very well. Or Celeste, for that matter. They were acquaintances at best."

"But you all ran in the same friend group from what I understand."

"A lot of kids run together. Doesn't mean we are best buds or anything." She runs a finger across the tabletop, rubbing at a smudge. I notice her fingernails are stained red.

"How did you get that red on your fingers?"

Her head snaps up and she puts her hands on her lap. "How do you think? I work with red frosting."

I look toward the display of donuts in the glass counter. Sure enough, one section has red, white, and blue frosting on them.

She laughs out loud, an angry sound. "Did you think that

was blood?" She spreads her hands on the table for me to see clearly. "Yeah, I killed two girls I barely know and didn't even wash my hands."

I'm growing to dislike this girl. She's all blond smiles behind the counter, but she has a mean streak.

"Did you?" I ask seriously. "You know Val, and know the woods near her house are remote. It would make sense."

Her face grows pained, and she leans forward across the table. "Are you serious right now?" she says in a broken voice.

"You tell me."

She looks away toward the floor, unable to meet my eyes.

"Please leave before I call the police and have you arrested for threatening me." She looks up from the floor. "I'm only seventeen, you'd go in for harassing a child."

I sit back in my seat and take a gentler tone. "I'm not harassing you. I'm just asking you a question."

"The answer is no. Maybe I wasn't very close to Celeste and Marie, but they were sort of friends. And they were brutally murdered." She sniffles a little. "Now you come here to my work and accuse me of doing those horrible things to them." Her voice cracks again.

The manager, Eileen, who I've known as a friend of Val's for many years, looks up when Kimmie's voice raises. A few patrons nearby eye us curiously. One of them whispers to her companion. I hear the words "ghost hunter."

I suddenly want to escape.

"Rylan, Kimmie, everything okay?" Eileen asks, wiping her hands on her green apron.

"Everything's fine," I say, feeling many pairs of eyes on me.

"Yeah. Sorry," Kimmie says. "I guess I got carried away."

What am I doing here? Maybe Kimmie's right, and I'm just harassing a young girl that has been through enough.

Kimmie tightens her apron and looks sad. "Are we done

here? Or is there something else you want to accuse me of?" she asks in a too-loud whisper.

A few gasps go up around the room.

I feel my face burning and I want to sink into the floor.

"I'm sorry," I mutter and, feeling foolish for coming, I let myself outside.

My mom's Cadillac has grown warm sitting in the sun outside The Hole. I sit in the heat, wondering where to go next. The bear claw sits heavily in my stomach, mixes with the uncertainty about what to do next.

I suddenly remember I didn't ask Kimmie about the coins. There's no way she'll talk to me now. The coins have to mean something big.

Why would someone put a strange coin into the mouth of a victim? In Celeste's case, the coin was put there while she was alive. It's what killed her. What does that mean?

If the symbols are Wiccan, I need to talk to a Wiccan.

I suddenly remember a flyer I picked up at the last paranormal fair that Mickey and I attended in Indianapolis. Having a booth at those kinds of fairs is not my favorite marketing strategy, but it does garner us a slew of new viewers and a few clients. Plus, Mickey enjoys talking to the fans. She runs the business end of the show and she says it's good to go.

I don't like the attention, but I do it for Mickey.

The White Witch, as she called herself, had a booth across the aisle from us. I spent a lot of time staring at her banner full of stars and moons. At one point in the day, I wandered over and picked up a flyer. The purple and black paper listed her services, which included "readings" and "charms and spells." If anyone knew what the coins mean, it would be her.

Now I just have to find the flyer. I lean over the back of the seat and dig through the layers of papers, junk mail, and fast-food wrappers that clog the footwells. I'm pretty sure I left the flyer in the car. I leave a lot of stuff in the car.

A corner of purple glittered paper peeks out from a pile, and I grab it eagerly.

I call the number on the flyer to make an appointment. No one answers and I almost hang up. At the last moment, I decide to leave a message.

"Hi, this is Rylan Flynn with the show *Beyond the Dead*. I have some questions about coins with the symbols for air and earth and fire and water on them. I'm hoping you can shed some light on what they are for."

I pause, not sure how much to say on a message. "This is for a murder investigation," I add, then leave my phone number. I hang up quickly, feeling like a fool. What can this White Witch tell me that the police can't find out for themselves?

Except the police think they have their killer. Are they even still looking, or are they just making a case against Val?

I fiddle with the charms on my bracelet, wondering what to do next when my phone rings. It's the White Witch.

"I'm so glad you called me back." I touch the cross on my bracelet and say a quick prayer for the right words. "I'd like to ask you about a coin that was found at a crime scene."

"Yes, you mentioned murder. Are you working with the police?"

"Um, not exactly. Would it be possible to come visit you and we can talk?"

TWENTY-ONE

RYLAN FLYNN

At the paranormal fair, the White Witch had been dressed for the part in a flowing gown and long hair. Today, after hours, at her home-based shop, she's dressed in jeans and a button-up. Her hair is in a long braid held with a red scrunchie. If I didn't know who I was meeting, I'd never have recognized her.

"Hi, I'm Lorraine," the middle-aged woman says in greeting. She notices my surprise. "I know, you expected the dress and all that. Sorry, I didn't think I needed to do that for you. You're in the business, you know how it is."

"I get it." I look down at my sneakers, torn jeans, and black T-shirt. At the fair, I wore a pantsuit. Both of us look different.

I follow her through the shop full of candles and various trinkets for sale. She leads me through a beaded curtain to a sitting area in back. I imagine this is where she does her "readings." The setting is so cliché, I expect to see a crystal ball.

"Do you have the coins?" she asks, sitting in an old-fashioned wood chair with red velvet upholstery.

"I don't," I say, my hopes sinking. "The police have them. They are part of the evidence." She motions to the other chair and I sit.

"I assume this is about those two girls I saw on the news. Horrible business."

"Yes, they both had a coin in their mouth when found." I cross my legs, then uncross them, uncomfortable.

Lorraine reaches out and pats my knee in a soothing gesture. "You mentioned the symbols for air, earth, water, and fire? Did one have triangles with extra bottom lines on it? One right side up, the other in reverse?"

"Yes. I only saw them for a moment, but that's what I saw."

She touches the end of her braid in thought, pulls out the red scrunchie then returns it. "Interesting. And you said the other was just triangles?"

"That's right. Do you know what they mean?"

"Well, like you said, they are the four elements, but to have them on coins is very rare."

"Where would someone even get such a coin? Do you sell them here?" I look through the hanging beads into the shop area.

"Oh, dear, no." She flips the braid back over her shoulder. "As I said, they are very rare. I've only seen them in books."

"What are they?"

"Talismans, relics," she says dramatically. "They are used in rituals."

I sit up straighter. "The murder scenes looked like rituals. What kind of rituals would you use the coins in?"

She picks at a tiny piece of lint on her jeans. "That isn't really my realm of expertise. I deal in white magic. That is black magic." I can tell she knows more than she's saying.

"But you have an idea what the killer might be up to?"

Lorraine rubs at her knee. "Was there cutting? Blood?"

"Yes. The first victim only had superficial cuts and she choked to death on the coin in her mouth. I'm thinking that was accidental, that the killer was doing a ritual and it went wrong."

"And the second victim?"

"Lots of blood. The cuts were anything but superficial."

"Her throat was cut?"

"Yes. How did you know? That hasn't been on the news."

She suddenly stands and retrieves a book from the other side of the room. The leather binding on the heavy book is frayed. A few pages are loose and try to slide onto the floor. She slips them back in, then flips through until she comes to a full-page drawing.

"Like this?"

I look at the book. The drawing is in pencil, of a young woman tied to a tree with cuts on her arms and legs. Her throat is cut, too. "Exactly like that."

"This is bad," she says, looking at the picture, reading the page next to it.

"What is that?"

"This is a ritual to bring a soul back from the dead. It is very advanced. Not everyone would try something like this. It requires a lot of blood."

"And murder?"

"Here it says to stop cutting before the volunteer dies."

"Volunteer?"

"The 'victim' must volunteer to participate in the ritual. That's the only way it works."

"So Celeste volunteered and choked to death? I can understand that, but what about Marie, the second victim? Her friend had just died. She must have known how dangerous the ritual was."

"Maybe she did. Maybe she just got caught up in the excitement. Black magic can be very—let's say, seductive, intriguing. Even addictive."

"Addictive?"

"First you just dabble a little. It's exciting, invigorating. Then you need to do more advanced things for the same rush. It's like a drug."

I wonder if she's talking from experience.

She closes the book suddenly and hands it to me. "Show this to the police. Maybe it will help."

I take the book, holding it with only my fingertips. I don't want to touch the old leather cover, it gives me the shivers.

She ushers me back through the shop full of trinkets, incense, and candles. I carry the book carefully. "I'll make sure you get this back," I say before I go. "After Ford is done with it."

She looks at me with an intensity she hasn't had so far. "That will work out, too."

"What will?"

"You'll see. Just give it time."

I have an hour drive back to Ashby to ponder what she means by that last remark.

It is late afternoon when I return to Ashby. On my way, I called both the jail and Keaton trying to find out about Val. The jail said she can't get calls. Keaton didn't answer. I figure no news is not good news.

The book rides on the passenger seat. As I drive, my eyes keep drifting over to it. I don't like having it in my possession. Just looking at it gives me the creeps. I should tell Ford and Tyler what I found out. I try his number and it goes to voice-mail, too. Everyone is busy and I'm driving around town with a cursed book in my car.

The only other person I know that deals in curses is my dad. I make a quick turn and head toward his house. He must be worried sick over his sister being in jail. We can commiserate together, and maybe find out more about the sick ritual.

He's sitting on his front porch when I pull into the short driveway. He waves when he sees my car.

"For a moment, I forgot you were driving your mom's car. I thought Margie was stopping by," he says sadly when I join him on the porch. Mom's been gone for two years and they had divorced a year before that, but it's obvious he still carries a torch for her. The divorce wasn't his idea and he took it hard.

"It's just a car," I say awkwardly. I'm not used to seeing him so down. I join him on the porch swing and sink into the blue striped cushions.

"Do you have any news on Val?" Dad asks. "I tried calling her and Keaton but got nowhere."

"I haven't heard anything," I say, sitting the big leather book on the table next to his tea. "How was service this morning? Sorry I didn't make it."

He brightens. "No worries. I know you had a late night last night. There's always next week." He eyes the book. "What did you bring that here for?" he asks.

"It's a book on black magic."

"I can see that. I don't like having that here."

"I don't like having it either, but I'm hoping it will help solve the case and free Val."

I have his attention and he leans forward. With the tip of a finger, he flips the book open.

"On one of those pages is an illustration that could be a drawing of the crime scenes. I just went to visit a woman I met at the paranormal fair. Her name's Lorraine. She's a white witch and gave me the book. She said the coins are used in a ritual to bring back a departed soul."

Dad looks at me closely. "You be careful messing with this stuff. You've already seen what it can lead to."

"I have no intention of messing with black magic, but I think Celeste and Marie were into it." I tell him how I invited Marie's ghost last night and how she, too, had a coin in her mouth. Dad listens to my theory, thoughtfully.

"But who is behind the murders?"

"That's the question. The girls both followed the band, Loose Gravel, maybe they are into the black arts, too. They don't look the type, but you never know. They've ruled out her boyfriend, Drew, but I'm not so sure. Maybe he's into some freaky stuff."

Dad flips a few more pages until he comes to the illustration in question. "Jeez, is that what the scenes looked like?"

I don't look at the book. "Yes. Right down to being tied to a tree."

Dad reads a moment. "It says to use the oldest tree in the area. That tree we were next to was massive. I'm sure it was old. Who would know where that tree was?"

Val would know.

I push that thought away. My aunt messing with black magic is preposterous. Besides, whose soul would she be trying to bring back?

The only dead person she was close to was my mom. I don't see her luring young women to the woods to hurt them and bring my mom's soul back.

Especially since it is stuck in my house.

There was that boyfriend of hers that died in high school. Killed by a drunk driver, if I have the story right. Could Val be trying to bring him back?

I try to picture my aunt with a knife in her hand.

There's just no way. I'm more certain than ever Val is innocent. I can't even believe I'm thinking like this.

Could Drew have done it? Who else could it be?

Dad suddenly closes the book. "That's enough of that. You show this to Ford then get rid of it. I don't even like it being around you. Especially with how sensitive to the other realm you already are."

"I tried calling Ford, but he didn't answer. He was very clear on me not pursuing this case. I don't think he'll like what I have to tell him."

"He'll forgive you. He always does."

"What's that supposed to mean?"

"Even when you were kids and you'd tag along with Keaton and him. They'd be doing something and you'd get in the way and mess it up. Keaton would always be furious with you and Ford would stick up for you."

"I don't remember that."

"I do. It used to drive Keaton crazy."

"Was I really that much of a pain?"

"No more than any little sister. My point is, you have to tell Ford about this ritual. He'll get over you nosing around."

"He's probably down at the precinct." I stand up. "Do you have a plastic bag, or something? I know it's nuts, but I don't like touching the book."

"It's not nuts. That's your instincts protecting you."

Dad disappears into the house. I sit on the porch swing, staring across the grass, my mind racing.

Who would do this awful ritual? The big question.

Val is innocent, so how did blood get in her house?

Why would the girls volunteer to be tied to a tree and tortured?

Maybe Ford has gotten further along and I can coax some information out of him.

Dad returns with a plastic grocery bag and I slide the book in it. I feel better just having it out of sight.

"You know, those girls must have trusted whoever did this to them. Especially the second victim. Celeste didn't know what was coming, but Marie did. Who would she follow into the woods with a knife?"

Another question I don't have an answer to, but I intend to find out.

Before I drop off the book to Ford, maybe I'll try talking to the band again. They all have alibis for Celeste's murder, but would they lie for each other? Plus, I wonder if they've been cleared for Marie's. Either way, they knew Celeste and Marie. Maybe they can shed some light on the situation.

I really want to talk to Celeste's boyfriend, Drew. He has to know more than he's telling.

Or he's hiding something. That girl in the band could be covering for him.

This time, I put the book in my trunk. I shove it in next to a box of old clothes I meant to donate and a toolbox Mom always kept.

I shut the trunk with a satisfying *thunk*. I check the time. It's early evening on a Sunday. Where can I find Loose Gravel?

I pull up their website on my phone and see they are playing at a winery on the outskirts of Ashby right now.

I try calling Ford first, just in case I can palm the book off on him. He doesn't answer, as I expected.

It's been a long day. I could go for a glass of wine.

TWENTY-TWO

RYLAN FLYNN

For a Sunday evening, there are a lot of cars in the parking lot of the winery. I came here once with Mickey and Marco and some friends. But that was a long time ago. I've never come here alone.

I park far from the front door and begin walking up the long drive. Grapes grow on either side, stretching across the field into the setting sun. Wine in this region of Indiana is a fairly new venture and I'm surprised again at how well the winery is doing.

I can hear Loose Gravel playing as I walk. There is a large outdoor area with tables and benches that all face the stage. I find a spot on a bench and watch the band.

A waitress brings me a glass of strawberry wine and I nod along to the music, sipping. Now that I'm here, I wonder what I'm doing. Listening as Ford talked to the band at The Lock Up was one thing; approaching them myself, asking about murder, is quite another.

Two uniformed officers are patrolling the expansive grounds. One of them nods as he passes. The other stares openly. I recognize him from the crime scene. I'm sure he recognizes me, too.

Oh well, sipping wine is not a crime, no matter how he is looking at me.

The winery is an all-ages establishment and children play in the grassy areas. A group of teenagers stand nearby, sending me darting looks and whispering. A boy, about fifteen, is pushed my way. He looks at his friends and they urge him on.

I drink my wine and wait for the inevitable. This has happened before.

"Um, my friends want me to ask you if you're that chick from the ghost show on YouTube."

Other than his use of "chick" I'd normally appreciate being recognized. Mickey tells me it helps with promoting the show. But I'm in investigation mode right now.

"I'm Rylan Flynn from *Beyond the Dead*, yes."

He looks at his friends and they wave him on. "That's cool. Um, my friends wondered if you are here on a case?"

For a moment, I think they are talking about the murders, then I realize they mean a ghost case.

"I'm not. I'm just here to relax."

"So this place isn't haunted?"

I hadn't thought of that. I look around the gathering dark, at the lines of grape vines growing all around. This would be a good place to find a ghost if there was one nearby.

"I don't see anything now," I say, with what I hope is a winning smile.

"Cool. You'll let us know if you see something? We'd love to see a ghost."

I give a small chuckle at his enthusiasm. "I'll let you know, but don't count on it."

He looks serious. "Why are you here alone? I'd think you'd have lots of friends to hang out with."

God bless the way the young say exactly what they are thinking, even when it's not necessarily nice.

I sit up straight and try not to take it personally. "I'm just relaxing alone," I lie.

"Seems like a big celebrity would at least have your cameraman with you."

"She's a camerawoman, and, no, I'm not here with her." I'm starting to get annoyed by the young man. I look around him at the band, hoping he'll get the hint.

He doesn't. "A woman? How cool." He looks around us, like he expects Mickey to appear with camera in hand. "She meeting you later?"

I'm starting to lose my patience. "Look, I don't mean to be rude, but I'm trying to relax here. I appreciate you like the show, I truly do, but maybe you should return to your friends."

He looks back at the group staring at us, his face not as open and friendly as before. "I guess."

"I don't mean to be rude, really."

"Sure, I get it. Nice to meet you." He begins to slink away. His friends all start laughing. I get the distinct feeling they all heard what was said and are laughing at me. The young man rejoins his friends and I hear a not nice word being said about me.

I try not to take offense since I was a bit rude, after all.

Sipping my sweet wine, I put the young man out of my mind. I focus on the band, wondering if they are connected to the murders and how to find out. For someone who recently lost his girlfriend, Drew seems very into the music.

The band finishes their set as full dark falls. The area is illuminated with torches and overhead lights strung from posts. It's a lovely scene. One that I wish I could enjoy with someone.

I brush that thought away, too. The only someone I want is not interested, beyond thinking of me as a little sister. I should turn my sights on someone else.

That's a situation I will worry about later.

Now that it's time to talk to the musicians, I realize I have no idea what I should say. They don't owe me any answers, even if I knew what the questions were. I watch from my bench as they disperse into the crowd.

The bass player, the girl that defended Drew at the bar, is walking this way. At first, I think she's coming to talk to me, but she walks on by to the small building I'm sitting in front of.

I see the bathroom sign and sigh in relief. She disappears around the corner. This would be a good time to get her alone and ask her what she knows about Celeste and Marie, and who she thinks might have hurt them.

Or if she's covering for someone.

The bathrooms are in the back and the building is surrounded by lines of grapes, stretching into the fields, into the dark. Without the band playing, it is eerily quiet, the murmur of the crowd barely reaching this far.

A shadow moves between two rows of vines, stopping me in my tracks.

I stare into the dark. The night has grown cloudy and, beyond the circle of light from the building, it is pitch black. I see a flash of gold.

Something is there.

I'm drawn to the entrance of the field and peer in. "Who's there?"

The shadow materializes into a shape wearing a gold necklace with a horse charm blinking in the dim light. Above the necklace is a dark slash and lots of blood stains.

It's Marie.

I step into the vines and she turns away.

I follow. "Come back, Marie. I won't hurt you."

The ghost slips through the vines and I have to hurry to keep up. She looks over her shoulder, sees me following and slips to the next row.

I try to follow, but the vines hold me back. I search the dark field for her, but she's gone.

I'm alone in the field, in the dark. The lights of the winery are far to my left, reflected on the low clouds.

Something moves behind me and I spin. Another dark shape is moving down the row toward me. A shape I recognize, but haven't seen since I was young.

The thing locked in Keaton's room.

The first spirit I ever saw.

"You can't be here," I stammer. "You're not real."

The shadow grows arms and reaches for me. Something wraps around my wrist, pulls me down.

My wrist burns from the touch and I feel a rock under my knee as I fall to the ground.

I scream.

I pull my arm away.

The form looms over me, its mouth hanging open, so close I can smell the stench of its breath.

I cower away from the mouth and scream again.

The figure leans closer, the mouth opens wide. I try to pull away, but it holds me tight.

I squeeze my eyes shut, ready to be devoured.

Hands are suddenly on my shoulders, shaking me. "Ma'am, are you okay?"

I open my eyes and blink several times. The officer that seemed to recognize me earlier is shaking my shoulder.

I spin around, looking for the horrible thing that was attacking me. My wrist is still held, but instead of a black shadow hand, a vine is looped around my wrist.

I stare in disbelief. How did that get there?

I pull my hand out of the loop.

"Are you okay?" the officer repeats. "You can't be in here."

He helps me to my feet as I mumble, "I thought—I thought I saw someone." My mind scrambles for a plausible excuse about why I'm deep in the vineyard alone and screaming.

The officer does a quick search around us. "I don't see anyone. Why were you screaming?"

A shaky laugh bubbles out of me. "Was I that loud?"

"Yes. The band woman saw you come in here and told me. I was halfway down the row when you started calling out."

"I'm sorry. I guess my imagination got the best of me."

He studies my face in the dim light. "How much have you had to drink?"

"Only one glass. I swear I'm not drunk or anything."

He lowers his voice although we are alone in the field. "I saw you at the crime scene. You're that ghost hunter whose aunt killed those girls."

"Aunt Val did no such thing," I protest. "But, yes, I'm Rylan Flynn."

"If your aunt is innocent, do you think screaming in a field, causing a public disturbance is the best way to help her case?"

"I didn't mean to cause a disturbance. Besides, we're the only ones here, it's not really public." I stretch my arms wide.

"That's a matter of perspective. Come on, let's get back to the winery. Since you've been having a rough few days, I will just give you a warning, but the vineyard is off limits to customers."

"I understand." I trudge behind the officer, my eyes darting, on alert for the horrible thing that attacked me.

Or I thought attacked me.

I catch a quick glimmer of Marie a few rows over, but she disappears as soon as she sees me looking at her.

It's for the best. I can't exactly talk to her with the officer nearby.

When we exit the field, I'm ashamed to see a small crowd has gathered behind the bathroom building. The girl from the band looks relieved that I was caught. She stands with her bandmates, watching. All of them eye me suspiciously.

"Customers are not allowed in the vineyard," the officer says to the group. "Please obey the rules." He turns. "Got it?"

The band girl laughs, then catches herself and covers her mouth with her hand. My face burns. I feel like I've been caught being naughty in school and I'm being reprimanded in front of the class.

Not that that ever happened to me.

Any ideas I had for investigating are gone now. All I want to do is escape the scrutiny.

"I think I'll just go home," I tell the officer.

He nods solemnly.

With my head held high, I walk away from the scene.

When I'm safe in my car, I realize my wrist is still stinging. When I look, I see a handprint burned into my skin.

TWENTY-THREE

FORD PIERCE

My shoulders ache, my eyes are tired and my heart hurts from the long day. Any day that starts with a dead girl, whose life was taken way too soon, is a bad day. I'm finally leaving the precinct, when I get a chance to check my phone. I see a few missed calls from Rylan. She didn't leave a message, but I'm sure I don't want to hear what she has to say.

That woman is a menace.

So I'm slightly surprised when I find myself driving down her street. I could have called. Why didn't I just call?

I'm too tired to wonder and I park behind the boat of a Caddy in her driveway. There is a small pile of boxes on her front porch. I wonder if she's home. Maybe she's out and hasn't taken in her deliveries.

The sky has been overcast, but raindrops spatter on the windshield. The boxes will soon be wet.

I get out of the car and hurry to the front door and ring the bell. I'm startled by a dog's bark, then remember she is watching her aunt's dog.

Thinking of Val makes my heart sink. I don't want to believe a woman I've known most of my life is capable of that horror inflicted on the two girls, but I have no choice. The DNA test came back and it is Marie's blood in her house.

There's only one explanation, but I don't want to face it. There has to be a mistake somewhere.

Besides the dog barking, there is no answer at the door, so I ring again and add a knock. I know she's in there, her car is parked out front.

I look at the boxes and at the dark house. Has she gone out? Who is she with?

Why do I care?

After the happenings of the last few days, my instincts are on high alert. I fight the urge to peek in her windows to look for her. Besides, the curtains are drawn over them.

The dog barks again and I hear movement inside. Something crashes and I hear a "Holy flip."

A smile is suddenly on my face at her familiar expression. Rylan is home.

She opens the door a crack and looks out. "Ford, what are you doing here?"

"You called and it's on my way home."

It's not strictly on my way, but I won't quibble over details.

"No it's not," she says through the crack of the door.

"Either way, did you have something you needed to tell me? You called but didn't leave a message."

The soft drops of rain are picking up to a real downpour, but she doesn't invite me in, doesn't even open the door.

"I have something to show you. A book."

"A book about what?" I'm starting to feel like this was a bad idea. Raindrops fall on my head and run down my face. "Can I come in? I'm getting soaked out here."

She looks panicked for a moment. "I'll come out to the garage. The book is in my car, anyway." She shuts the door and I'm left alone on the porch, getting wet along with the boxes from UPS.

A moment later, the garage door opens and I hurry inside. There isn't much room to stand. The garage is full of furniture and boxes.

Rylan sees me looking at the stacks filling the garage. "Sorry about the mess," she says. "When I inherited the house, I just moved all my stuff from my apartment into the garage and I haven't gone through it yet.

"I understand." I really don't. Her mom died two years ago. That's plenty of time to clean out a garage. She looks ashamed of the stuff, so I don't push it. "So, what's this book you need to show me?"

Lightning snakes across the sky and thunder crashes a moment later. I feel the electricity in the air.

"Yeah, it's a book on black magic."

This is not at all what I expected to hear. "Where did you get a book on black magic?"

She smiles enigmatically. "From the White Witch."

I think she's joking, but she's serious. I shouldn't be surprised

"How about you just show me."

She finds a jacket on an overcrowded coat rack, puts it over her head and runs out into the rain. I stand just inside the garage where it is dry, wondering if I should follow her. She's back before I make up my mind.

"Here. I don't like having this, it makes me feel weird." She hands me a plastic grocery bag with something heavy in it.

I peer inside and see a large leather-bound book. "Black magic from the White Witch? Maybe you better explain before I touch it."

"What's to explain? It's a book on black magic. Doesn't everyone have one of those?" The corners of her mouth lift a little, softening her sarcasm.

Lightning slices through the air nearby, illuminating her

front yard like daylight for a moment. It's creepy to be holding such a book during a thunderstorm.

"Seriously. Where did you get it?"

"I visited a woman named Lorraine who calls herself the White Witch. I asked her about the coins and the way the girls were killed—"

I interrupt her. "You mean you were investigating?"

She looks at her bare feet. "Maybe. But look, I can't just sit here and do nothing while you guys are trying to put Val away for life."

My shoulders tighten and thunder rolls across town. "We're not trying anything. We're following the evidence. The murder weapon with Marie's blood is in her house. How do you explain that?"

She glares hard. "I don't know, yet."

I sigh heavily. "Okay. The book."

She reaches into the bag and pulls it out, opens it to a full-page illustration. "Look."

I suck in a breath. On the page is the same thing I've seen in the woods. The only difference is the clothes. The girl on the page is wearing a dress, Celeste and Marie were wearing jeans.

"What is that?"

"Lorraine says it is a ritual to bring a soul back from the dead. It has to be performed on a willing victim."

"Celeste and Marie volunteered to be killed?" I take the book and look it over closely. It's a horrible recipe for death right down to the coin in the mouth and the cuts on the arms and legs.

"I think Celeste was an accident. Maybe Marie didn't realize she was going to be killed, just cut. Maybe she got caught up in the excitement of doing something so dangerous and she didn't think of the consequences."

"But the killer knew. He didn't accidentally cut her throat."

She smirks and crosses her arms.

"What?" I ask.

"You said *he*. That means you don't think Val did it."

I snap the book shut and drop it back into the bag. "Fine. I don't really think she did it, but my hands are tied. You bring me some real evidence of her innocence, something I can use, and I'll gladly let her go. Until then, there's nothing I can do."

"Innocent until proven guilty. Does that ring a bell?"

I run a hand over my short hair. "The DNA on the knife proves her guilty. Not to mention she knew both girls and they were found on her property."

"That doesn't mean anything."

"That means everything." The storm picks up intensity and rain pounds just outside the open garage door, splashes in on our feet. We stand there staring each other down. I hold her blue eyes, wait for her to look away.

She holds my gaze, daring me.

I suddenly feel foolish. I let my eyes slide to the storm outside. It's really coming down, but I want to leave.

"Thanks for the book," I say lamely. "I'll look into it more tomorrow."

"Thank you," she says with genuine appreciation. "Please, promise me you won't stop looking for the real killer."

This girl is like a dog with a bone and won't let go.

"I promise. Now will you promise to stop snooping around and doing my job."

She smiles prettily. "You know I can't promise that."

"Rylan Flynn, you are the most exasperating person I have ever met."

Her smile widens. "That's what I'm trying for. Seriously, look into the people both girls might have trusted enough to be led into the woods."

"We've been working that angle all day. We haven't gotten too far."

"I thought it might be the band, or something related to the band."

She looks at the ground and I can tell she's hiding something. "What did you do?"

"I didn't do anything. I didn't know what to do once I got there."

"Got where?"

"I went to the winery where they were playing tonight. I didn't talk to them, but I wanted to."

"You're not telling me something."

She toes the wet floor, leaving little prints on the concrete. "I'm sure you'll hear about it, so I might as well tell you. I went into the vineyard because I saw Marie's ghost. I followed her, but she got away."

"And?"

"And I got scared and might have started screaming. One of the officers on security duty had to come get me out of the field."

The thought of Rylan alone and screaming in a field makes my stomach hurt. "Why were you screaming?"

She focuses on the floor, rubs her bare toes through the water. "I don't know how to explain it. I thought I saw something."

Seeing things is what she does for a living. Whatever she saw in that field must have been awful. She obviously doesn't want to tell me what it is.

"You okay now?"

She rubs her wrist and says, "Yeah, I'm good now. I'm only telling you now so you're not mad in the morning if someone talks about it at the precinct."

"You having a run-in with the police is hardly news anymore," I tease.

Her head snaps up and she looks ready to tell me off. I smile and she relaxes. "I suppose you're right."

The rain has let up some and I've been up since yesterday. "Look, I'm going to go. Thanks again for the book."

"Sure. Hope it helps." She looks like she wants to say something.

"What is it?" I ask gently.

"Have you seen Val? Is she okay?"

"I want to see her, but Keaton has advised her not to talk to us."

She nods sadly. "I haven't been able to talk to her either. She'll be okay, right? No one will hurt her or anything?"

I wish I could tell her everything will be fine, that Val is safe and happy. "Jail's not pretty," I say.

She looks me straight in the eye, and I feel like I'm pinned to the ground. "Then get her out."

I don't want to argue the point again, so I say my goodbyes and head into the rain. Rylan watches from the garage as the wipers furiously clear my windshield. The book sits on the front seat.

I hope I will find something helpful in it.

I hope the killer isn't reading it now, getting ideas.

TWENTY-FOUR

The raging storm hides the moon, but I know it is still full. I can feel it like a pressure on my skin.

"You're running out of time," the painting tells me. "It has to be during a full moon."

I don't want to listen to the painting, so I go to the room. I close the door tight behind me and shiver and cover my nose.

I've turned the AC to max and it is cold in here. Really cold.

But that hasn't stopped the smell.

Her body lies in the middle of the room where I dragged it the day I found her dead.

"Found dead?"

Her face is dark purple, her fingers are shriveled. She wasn't a small woman in life, now her abdomen is bloated.

I've placed two-liter bottles of frozen water around her to ward off decomposition, but the bottles have thawed.

"Stupid child. You need to fix this," I hear between rolls of thunder.

I collect the bottles and return them to the large freezer in the garage. I have another set waiting and I repack her body with them.

The bottles amuse me. In life, she never allowed me to drink soda. After she died, I drank gallons of it and saved the bottles. The colorful labels surrounding her discolored skin make me smile.

The altar against one wall holds burned-out candles. I replace the guttered stubs of wax with fresh black ones. I say a prayer to the dark one, the way she taught me, as I light a match.

But I pray too slowly and the match burns down to my fingertips before I get the candle lit.

A laugh fills the room. "You singed yourself, didn't you? I can't even trust you to light a candle."

I swing around, ready to defend myself. "I can light a candle. I can do lots of things. I framed that woman so they think she did it."

"The first smart thing you've done."

The contorted, discolored face of the corpse smiles. An empty Pepsi bottle full of frozen water leans against her cheek. I smile back.

Thunder shakes the house, and rain pelts the curtained windows as I try again. Candlelight wavers across the leather book open on the altar.

"You must try again. This time, you need someone special."

"I have someone in mind. Just you wait. She's perfect."

"Don't screw it up." Maniacal laughter, reminiscent of when I'd get in trouble and I'd get my "special punishment" in the corner of the room.

I turn my back on her dead body and look at the book. I must be missing something in the ritual, some small detail must be wrong. I flip through the pages, searching for anything that will help bring her soul back.

The burning candle catches my attention.

Fire.

I need to add fire to the blood.

And use the special girl.
The other girls weren't right, they were weak.
Tomorrow, before the moon shifts, is my last chance.

TWENTY-FIVE

RYLAN FLYNN

I went to sleep frustrated with Ford and, after a night of awful dreams of Val being tortured in jail, I awake angry.

And a little afraid.

What if we never find the real killer? What if Val goes down for this?

Who is framing her for the murders and why?

Despite Ford's warnings about staying out of it, I can't let go. With a renewed sense of purpose, I climb out of bed and across the clothes clogging my floor.

I need coffee.

George hurries down the hall so fast he stumbles and bounces off the wall, into the stack of boxes in front of Keaton's old room.

For a moment, the terror of the dark figure attacking me last night takes my breath away. Images of the shape grabbing my arm fill my mind.

"Stay away," I yell to the door and frantically restack the boxes. I hug the far wall as I pass the door.

"Rylan, are you okay? I thought I heard you yelling," Mom says. I'm surprised to see her.

"I'm fine, Mom." I lean against her doorjamb. I wish I could tell her all about what's going on. I wish she would understand. Sometimes having her here is harder than the loss of her. She's here, but not here.

I should help her cross over.

I'm not ready to let go yet.

"Did you eat?"

I smile at the usual question. "Not yet. I'm going to get something at The Hole."

"Nice. Tell Val I said hi."

"I will," I lie. Even if Val was there, Mom's visits are a secret I keep.

George pushes against my hand, wanting to go out. Mom's eyes widen when she sees him. "Did you get a dog?" Her face scrunches in confusion.

"Just babysitting him for a few days."

"Oh." She begins brushing her hair, always brushing her hair. I wonder if that was what she was doing when someone snuck into this house and shot her. I found her on the bed, not under the covers. Maybe she was sitting on the side like she is now, brushing her hair when...

I don't want to think about it.

"I need to let the dog out," I tell her, hurrying down the crowded hall and away from the painful memory.

Monday mornings are much slower than the crush of the Sunday-after-church crowd. By the time I get there, the shop is empty except for Eileen.

"How's Val?" she says when I walk up to the counter. "This is just all so horrible what they said she did. I know our Val would never, never do such a thing," Eileen gushes in her usual overly chatty way.

"I haven't been allowed to talk to her. I'm hoping she will be released soon, though."

"How horrible. Just horrible. I can't even imagine what she's going through." Eileen's worried expression hurts my heart. "How you holding up? You doing okay with all this?"

"I'm doing fine." I rub at the finger marks on my wrist that still sting. "Can I get a bear claw and a coffee?"

"Of course, of course. Here I am prattling on and you're hungry." She hurries to get my order. I feel bad for making her serve me, but my stomach is rumbling. She refuses to charge me, so I drop a few dollars into her tip jar.

Eileen rubs her hands down her green apron with The Hole logo on the front. "Look, things are super quiet this time in the morning. I need to run to the post office. I know you are busy and probably have things to do, but with all that's happened, I haven't done it yet. Do you think you could watch the counter for just a bit? Today is normally my day off, but I came in to open for Val. I really hate to ask, but could you?"

I occasionally work the counter when Val is short-handed and I don't mind at all. I don't have to be anywhere for at least an hour, when I need to be at Mickey's.

"I don't mind." I duck around the counter and pull an apron off a hook in the hall.

"You're a life saver, truly you are. I'll be right back. Hopefully there isn't a line." She grabs her purse from under the counter. "Oh, I sure hope not. Now I'll be back in a flash. It's been quiet, so don't you worry about that."

"Take as long as you need." I take a bite of the bear claw. "This is delicious, by the way," I say around a mouthful.

Eileen beams. "Thank you. Your aunt's recipe you know," she says, then she's gone out the door.

I stand awkwardly behind the counter in the empty store. I eat the bear claw and drink my coffee, thinking.

No customers come, which is good, because I have a plan.

Kimmie knew Celeste and she knew Marie. She's involved with the band.

All of that seems too coincidental.

A sinking suspicion creeps into my mind. She also knows Val and where Val lives. She knows about the woods.

Could she have done these horrible things?

The bear claw flips in my belly. Could she?

I need proof.

I run to the front door and check the sidewalk to be sure Eileen isn't coming back yet. The coast is clear.

I hurry to the back room where the employee lockers are. Maybe there is something in Kimmie's locker that will give me a clue.

The lockers are unlocked. It only takes two wrong choices until I find one that looks like Kimmie's. There's a few hair ties and a small makeup bag inside. I take the bag out and zip it open.

Inside is an eyeliner and something shiny. I pull the shiny thing out and it is a necklace.

With a horse charm.

Exactly like the ones both Celeste and Marie were wearing.

"This can't be a coincidence," I say to the empty back room.

Only, it's not empty.

"I was afraid someone would come looking in my locker," Kimmie says. "I should have known it would be you. You have to have your nose in everyone's business."

I look up like I've been caught stealing. I drop the little makeup bag and it rattles on the tile floor.

Kimmie and her friend from the bar, Tabitha, are filling the doorway, both looking furious. Kimmie bends to pick up the bag. Tabitha takes the necklace from my hand. I notice a similar chain peeking from the collar of her shirt.

"My mother always said, 'girls that ask questions get into trouble'," Tabitha says.

I look at the two girls and try to imagine them as the killers.

"You should see your face," Kimmie laughs. "Seriously. It took you long enough to figure it out."

"I don't think she has figured it out yet," Tabitha says, walking slowly around me, studying me.

"Figure what out?"

"We need *you* to make the ritual work."

I back away from the girls and knock into the small table in the break room.

"You don't want me. I won't volunteer. You need someone to volunteer to be the victim."

Both sets of eyes grow wide. "How do you know that?" Kimmie asks.

"I've read the book. I know all about the ritual to bring back a soul. I just don't know whose soul you are trying to bring back." I shuffle around the table and keep backing up until I reach the far wall. The girls block the only door. I'm trapped.

"You'll meet her soon enough," Tabitha says.

Suddenly, both girls tackle me and I hit the tile hard.

Tabitha holds my hair and slams my head into the floor. Kimmie is on my legs. I kick at her, but can't get her off. "I've got the tape," she says.

The unmistakable sound of duct tape unrolling fills the room and she binds my ankles together. The tape is so tight, it cuts into my skin.

"What are you doing?" I wriggle, but Tabitha's weight is on my chest. I'm finding it hard to breathe.

I wish desperately that Eileen would return and catch them in the act. What is taking so long at the post office?

"We better hurry," Kimmie says, breathless. Tabitha takes the tape from her and flips me onto my belly. Each girl grabs an arm and pulls it behind my back. My face is smashed into the tile. From here, I can see a dead bug under the lockers along with a few dust bunnies. I wonder if it is one of the last things I will ever see.

One of the girls grabs my hair and pulls my head up. Duct tape suddenly covers my mouth.

I scream against the tape, desperately hoping Eileen will walk in the door and save me from these two killers.

Eileen where are you?

"You freaked me out yesterday when you insinuated I had something to do with Celeste and Marie," Kimmie says near my ear after bending down. "Too bad you fell for my sad act and didn't realize you were right."

"Help me carry her," Tabitha says. "We need to get out of here."

The girls pick me up. I wriggle and fight and they drop me on the floor with a thud.

Tabitha takes a knife from her pocket and flips it open. "Either come with us quietly, or I'll cut you." She has a horrible gleam in her eye and I realize she's the one that cut the girls.

I nod, helpless, as they carry me out the back door to their car in the alley.

I can't believe this is happening in broad daylight. I want to fight, but Tabitha has the knife and seems eager to use it. I let them put me in the backseat and hope Eileen will call the police when she sees I'm not at the shop.

Taking their seats in the front, the girls giggle and congratulate each other. My hands are squashed underneath me and are already beginning to go numb from being taped so tightly. I struggle against the tape and Kimmie turns around in the passenger seat.

"You might as well enjoy the ride. It's the last one you will ever take."

I scream at her in my throat, the tape blocking the sound.

"Ha, she sounds like Celeste," Tabitha says. "Don't worry. It will all be over before long. As soon as the moon comes out, the fun will begin."

It's only late morning, the moon is far away. I pray more fervently than I've ever prayed that I can find a way to escape before then.

TWENTY-SIX

RYLAN FLYNN

The girls, the monsters, discuss my fate as they drive. From what I gather, they intend to repeat the ritual they did with Celeste and Marie. Only this time they intend to add some things to make it work. The addition makes me squirm.

"I think the fire will do the trick," Tabitha says.

"I don't know. What if someone sees it? Besides, the book doesn't say to use fire."

"The book is just a guideline," Tabitha says sulkily. "I think it's what we need to bring her back." She looks over her shoulder. I put all my fury into my eyes. Hers are black and flat, terrifying. "Besides," she adds, turning back to the road, "it will be fun."

I expect Kimmie to be disgusted at this, but she laughs and turns to look, too. "Can't wait to see it work. All this trouble and Tabitha's mom is still rotting away." She is so casual about my death she might as well be talking about a shopping trip.

Tabitha's mom? Is that who they are trying to bring back?

My bound hands are nearly numb and aching badly. I shift on the seat and try to sit up. Kimmie sees me wriggling.

"Stay down," she growls.

I've managed to get my head up to the window and peer out. Tabitha flicks her eyes over her shoulder. She suddenly turns, her fist flying at my face.

I turn my head just in time to save my nose. The blow catches me on the temple. The car lurches to the right, tossing me against the door.

"I said stay down. Didn't your mom teach you to listen?" she shouts. "You nearly made me lose control of the car."

My head rings from the punch, my eyes stinging. I can't cry, can't give in. If my nose gets stuffed, I won't be able to breathe.

Kimmie turns completely around, grinning wildly as I slide down the door to the seat. "Good girl," she says. "Too bad. I wanted to hit you, too." She leans over the back of the seat. "I'll get my chance."

I cower and sink into the seat, shocked at the girls' violence.

We soon turn onto gravel. A driveway. It must be long, because we crunch along for several moments. Out the windows, trees loom, branches scraping along the roof of the car.

We finally park and the girls get out. I brace for attack as the door opens and they grab my legs.

"Now be good and I won't cut you." Tabitha says, the knife in her hand.

"You'll be good, won't you?" Kimmie asks.

I nod helplessly, staring at the glint of the knife. I'm hauled out of the car and dragged along grassy gravel. I look all around, trying to figure out where they took me.

We are on an old farm, the grass high, the gravel choked with weeds.

They carry me onto a wide covered porch and drop me to the floor. My hip aches where it lands on the wooden planks.

Tabitha messes with a ring full of colorful keychains, searching for the key to the front door. I toy with the idea of wiggling away, rolling down the front steps.

With my feet and hands taped, I won't get far.

I sit still, focusing on breathing out my nose. Sniffling a little, and trying not to panic about it.

After what seems like a long time, the door finally swings open.

A slightly sour smell wafts out.

"Ooh," Kimmie says. "We need to change the ice again."

Tabitha looks perturbed at the mention of the smell. "I just did it this morning."

Kimmie waves a hand in front of her nose. "Won't matter after tonight." She roughly shoves her hands under my arms and drags me inside the farmhouse.

She dumps me on a red and blue braided rug at the base of the stairs, just inside the door. "Where do we put her until the moon comes out?" Kimmie asks.

Tabitha grins. "The cage."

I don't like the sound of that. I squeal against the tape. Tabitha puts the knife to my throat. "You want cut?" The tip of the knife pokes into my skin. I shake my head, a tiny movement. She shuts the knife and puts it in her pocket, then grabs my feet.

"Help me carry her upstairs," she says.

Tabitha again shoves her hands under my arms and they struggle to carry me up the stairs directly in front of the front door. At the top of the stairs, they set me down, both of them panting.

"Jeez, lay off the donuts, why don't you," Kimmie snarks.

The smell is stronger up here. Something sour lies behind one of the doors.

"Good thing we are doing this today," Kimmie says. "She's getting ripe."

Tabitha lurches at Kimmie, shoves her against the plaster wall so hard that dust falls from a crack.

"Stop that. She's fine. She has to be fine. Get it?"

Kimmie looks scared, but quickly hides it. "I'm sorry. Of course she's fine. I was just saying."

"Saying what?"

Kimmie looks at the red flowered carpet. "Nothing."

"That's what I thought." Tabitha opens a door, then grabs my ankle. "Ready?"

Together they lift me and take me through the open door.

Inside, it is freezing. A window air conditioner is running full blast. Goosebumps break out on my arms. My nose is assaulted by the stench of decay mixed with something floral like air freshener.

They drop me on the floor and I land on my side. I see what is making the smell.

A dead woman is rotting in the middle of the room, her face inches from mine.

I scream against the tape and try to wriggle away.

"Stop that!" Tabitha kicks me in the ribs. "You show my mother some respect or I'll kill you now."

I stop screaming, and turn my head away from the woman.

"You'll get to know her really well today," Kimmie says with glee. Behind me, metal rattles. "You have the key?" she asks Tabitha.

Out comes the keyring with the colorful keychains. I maneuver around so I can see what they are unlocking.

A metal cage is in the corner. A chain and a lock hold it closed.

I push against the carpet with my feet, desperate to get away.

I only make it a few inches when Tabitha grabs hold of my ankle and pulls me to the cage. "You'll like it in here. I've spent hours in the cage. It did me good. Taught me to follow Mom's rules." She looks at the body on the ground. "Plus, it's what she would want."

I shake my head and yell against the tape. I don't care if Tabitha cuts me. I don't want to be locked in that cage.

I kick both legs and she drops my ankle.

"I warned you," Tabitha says and the knife flashes. She slices it down my shoulder.

The pain brings me to my senses, makes me freeze in obedience.

I try not to cry, sniffing as hard as I can to keep my nose clear.

With the knife so close to my throat, I can't stop them from shoving me into the cage. There's barely room to lie on my side with my knees bent. It was obviously built for a smaller person.

A child.

A rush of sympathy for Tabitha fills me, despite the cut on my shoulder and the nick on my neck from the tip of the knife.

If she was locked in this cage as a child, no wonder she is unstable.

Once the lock is secured and they know I can't escape, they seem to forget I'm here.

They both kneel by the body and murmur what might be prayers, but not to God.

Then, in unison, they stand and approach what looks like an altar, say more words, maybe an incantation, and light the candles.

I watch in awe and disgust. The entire situation is perverse. The looks of deep devotion on both their faces disturb me. As they continue chanting, I have to look away.

I bury my face against the back bars of the cage and say my own prayers.

I'm so intent on praying to the true God for help, I don't realize they have stopped until the door shuts behind them.

I am alone with the dead woman.

I instantly try to free my hands. My shoulders ache

painfully from being in this awkward position. The cut stings. My wrists are raw from pulling at the tape.

Still, I try.

And the rectangle of light on the floor travels across the red flowered carpet, growing closer to night. To the moon. To the ritual.

I grow increasingly uncomfortable. My hands are completely numb, as are my feet. My legs ache from being cramped and bent awkwardly. My tongue feels thick and dry and I struggle to swallow.

Worst of all, I need the restroom. The pressure has grown to the point I'm afraid I may mess myself here in this cage.

"Please," I beg the empty room.

And she appears.

The ghost of Tabitha's mother stands before the cage.

"What has that girl done now?" she asks.

The ghost leans close to the cage, scrutinizes me.

"This isn't good," she says. She stands tall, then suddenly lunges toward me.

I flinch.

She gasps in surprise. "You can see me?"

I nod enthusiastically.

"Interesting." She looks at her body on the floor. "How long have I been like that?"

I can't answer, so I shake my head.

"Right. The tape." She bends to inspect her body. "This is just wrong. I don't deserve this."

The woman seems totally normal. It's hard to believe she locked her daughter in this cage. Hard to believe she raised a monster—a murderer.

"Why are you here? What does she plan to do with you?"

I widen my eyes, try to ask for help. She turns away.

She runs a hand along the altar with the same rapt, devoted face the girls had.

She's a believer. Probably taught Tabitha all she knew. Maybe even taught Kimmie and the other girls.

On her wrist, I see a tattoo of a horse, similar to the charm on the girls' necklaces.

She bends and looks at the open book. "Oh, Tabitha, is that what you're doing?" She looks at me, seriously. "You don't look like a volunteer. This will never work." She shakes her head and reaches to turn a page.

Her hand goes through the book. "Oops, forgot I'm not really here."

I shift uncomfortably against the bars and she looks to me. "It's not so bad if you stay still. My mom taught me that."

I'm sickened to think this woman was tortured in this cage the same as Tabitha. The cage is full of sadness, it clings to the bars, hurts my heart.

My heart that races painfully.

I breathe deeply through my nose to calm it, wish desperately the tape on my mouth was gone.

The ghost looks at me, curious. "She did a good job tying you up. Is it bad?" There's a little flicker of enjoyment in her eyes, and I get a glimpse of what life with her as a mother must have been like.

"If I could help you, I would." She doesn't sound like she would help me. She's getting a sick satisfaction out of seeing me tied and caged.

"Still, when Tabitha gets caught, and that stupid girl will for sure get caught, that could be a disaster for her." She leans close to the bars. "I can't let that happen."

She suddenly stands tall, her head cocked as if she's listening.

Downstairs has been quiet except for the TV playing all afternoon. Now the sound of knocking on the front door comes through the floor.

"We have a visitor," the ghost says, and she disappears.

TWENTY-SEVEN

FORD PIERCE

For the second night in a row, I dream of Rylan being tortured.

And it puts me in a bad mood.

Not that I would be in a good mood with this investigation gnawing at me. By the afternoon, I'm hungry and tired and ready for a break from my desk.

No break is coming.

My desk phone rings.

"Pierce," I say.

"Detective, there is someone here to see you," the front desk tells me. "He says he's Celeste Monroe's boyfriend."

"Drew or Andy?"

"Drew."

"I'll be right there." I return the phone to the cradle and look at Tyler. "Drew from the band is here. Want in?"

"You know it."

We walk to the front lobby where Drew waits nervously.

"Drew, good to see you again. This is Detective Spencer."

They shake hands.

"Let's talk in a room," Tyler says, leading the young man down the hall.

Once we are settled at the table, I ask, "What can we do for you?"

Drew pulls on the hem of his T-shirt. "I don't know if this will help with the investigation into who killed Celeste, but I wanted you to know about the group she's in."

"Group? Like a band?" Tyler asks.

"Not that kind of group. Some girls from the school are in it." He sighs and sits back in his chair. "She joined a few weeks ago when she moved here."

"To be with you," Tyler points out.

"Yes, to be with me. At least, I guess."

I wonder if he knows about Celeste's man on the side.

"I can't help feeling responsible in some small way." He looks over my shoulder and swallows hard, trying to keep his emotions in check.

"It's okay. Take your time," I tell him.

"She told me a short time after she got here about the new group she joined. At first, I thought she was joking. I mean, the name alone sounds made up."

"What was the name?"

"The Coven of the Caballo. You know, the Spanish word for horse. I mean, come on, caballo?"

I sit back in my chair, not sure what to think of this information. "What did this group do? Ride horses together?"

"No. That's what I thought at first." Drew leans forward, lowers his voice. "I think it was a witchcraft thing."

Like the ritual in the book. I sit forward, all attention now.

"Celeste was into witchcraft?"

"I mean, I think so. That's what she hinted at, anyway. She didn't come right out and say it, but I got the feeling some of her friends were playing around with spells and things. I didn't think too much of it until I learned how she died." Drew's voice breaks. "If I had known it would lead where it did, I would have gotten involved, or at least told her to stop." He looks at the floor. "I thought they were just girls messing around. Plus, we've been super busy with the band."

"Do you know which other girls are involved in this coven?" Tyler asks.

He looks up. "A few girls I've seen around. That Kimmie Steele and her friend Tabitha Lipinsky. I think that Marie girl that was killed was also in on it."

"We found a necklace on Celeste and Marie with a horse charm on it. Do you know the necklace? Does that mean anything to you?"

"Celeste got it recently. She never took it off. I suppose that could have to do with the coven thing. Like I said, I really didn't pay much attention. We just wrote some new songs and I've been covered up with rehearsals."

I'm starting to see why Celeste strayed with Andy.

I look to Tyler and can tell he's itching to look into this new lead. "Drew, thanks for coming and thanks for the information. We will look into it," he says.

Drew stands and shakes our hands. "Just find whoever did this to Celeste."

We promise to do all we can. Then we head out to visit Kimmie Steele and Tabitha Lipinsky.

A quick call to the school reveals both girls skipped today. Curious.

No one is home at Kimmie's house, so we move on to Tabitha's. Her mother, Agatha, lives out on County Road 11. We go there first.

The rundown farmhouse sits way back off the road, and we drive for several moments down weed-choked gravel.

"Doesn't look like anyone's lived here for a while," Tyler comments.

"Or they just let the place run down," I point out. "There's a car in the drive."

A dark-blue sedan is parked by the porch. Insects sing in the trees when we get out. The front porch sags a little on the left and has peeling paint.

I follow Tyler up the porch steps and he bangs on the front door. Inside the house, we can hear the TV playing.

No one answers the first knock, but the TV shuts off.

Tyler knocks again. "Ashby Police Department," he says.

The door opens a crack. A young woman I recognize from The Lock Up as Tabitha peers out. "Can I help you?" she asks through the crack.

"Tabitha, we need to talk to you about something. Can we come in?"

She opens the door a few more inches but doesn't let us in. "What's this about?" she demands.

"Is your mother home?" Tyler asks.

"She's not well. She's upstairs sleeping."

I want to catch her off guard, so I ask, "Have you heard of a group called the Coven of the Caballo?"

Her face flashes pale, then turns pink. "I've never heard of it."

"Can we come in?" Tyler asks again. "It will only take a moment."

She steps back and the door swings in. She backs into the foyer and stands at the base of the stairs.

"What is this about again?" she asks, all sweetness and sunshine. I don't buy the act.

"This is about Celeste Monroe and Marie Prestwood. We heard from a source that you were in a group together with both girls. A coven of sorts," I say.

"That's silly. A coven? You mean witchcraft?"

"We do." Tyler says. "Do you know anything about it?"

"How would I? It's not like Celeste and Marie were good friends or anything. I knew them, saw them around at shows and stuff. But we weren't in any group together."

I see a glimmer of chain around her neck. "Can I see your necklace?"

Her face turns even more pink. "My necklace?"

"The girls in the group all wore horse charm necklaces. So did Marie and Celeste. Can I see your necklace, please?"

She reluctantly lifts the chain from her collar. A golden horse charm dangles on it. "My m-mother g-gave me this," she stammers.

"It's just like the others. That's quite a coincidence," Tyler says.

"And I'm done talking to you. Unless you have a warrant or something, I'd like it if you leave."

"And we'd like to talk to your mother," I say.

"I told you. She's upstairs very ill. Not sure if she will make it or not at this point."

I search her face for lies; something in her eyes makes warning bells go off in my mind. She's right, though, we have no legal right to continue questioning her.

"She needs to rest. It's better if you go," she says, ushering us to the door.

A movement at the top of the stairs catches my eye. A shadowy figure lurks there.

Tabitha sees me looking and darts her eyes to the steps. She must not see the shadow shape. When she turns her eyes back, she seems relieved. "Detectives?" she motions to the door.

I look back up the stairs. The figure has gained more form and looks like a woman.

A ghost.

"Sorry to bother you," Tyler says, all professional, but without warmth. We both know something is going on.

"No bother. I hope you find out who killed those girls. So tragic," Tabitha says. There's a bothersome glint in her expression. She seems to be enjoying this.

Tyler hands her a business card. "Call me if you want to tell us anything. Anything at all."

She takes the card with the tips of two fingers, holds it away from her like it's contaminated. "I will," she lies.

I look back up the steps. The figure is gone.

I'm not thinking of Tabitha and her obvious lies as we drive away. I'm only thinking of one thing.

Did I just see a ghost?

TWENTY-EIGHT

RYLAN FLYNN

Muffled voices talk downstairs. In my desperate state, I imagine it is Ford coming to rescue me. But no rescue comes.

Tires on gravel fade away.

The TV comes back on.

"No, come back," I scream against the tape. Barely a sound comes out.

I collapse against the bars of the cage, sniffling furiously against the threat of smothering to death from a stuffed nose.

I'm beginning to grow frantic about my nose. I rub my face against my shoulder trying to wipe it. I can only rub my chin and a little of my lips. The edge of the tape sticks to my shirt and a few inches pull up. I can open my mouth a little on the right.

I breathe deeply from the slit, long slow breaths.

The panic in my chest subsides.

I squirm uncomfortably against the pressure in my bladder, almost to the point of not caring if I make a mess or not.

I may be dead soon anyway.

Why not leave them a mess to clean up.

A mixture of relief and shame fills me as my jeans grow damp.

A deep hatred of the girls takes over the shame. They drove me to this.

With renewed vigor, I try to free my hands, pulling painfully on the tape. They wrapped my wrists tight. I manage a little wiggle room, but they won't come apart.

I push my legs against the bars of the cage, hoping to knock one loose. The cage holds.

I scream with frustration and rage, and an edge of panic. I need out of this cage now. I need my hands free. I need to be released.

I scream against the tape until my throat hurts, then I scream some more.

The door to the room opens and Kimmie comes in. "Almost time. The moon is out. Are you excited?"

Tabitha follows her into the room and approaches the cage. She looks inside and sees the mess I've made.

"You sick animal," she says, her face filling with rage.

Kimmie looks into the cage too, begins to laugh. "What a child. Couldn't you just hold it?"

I make a sound of frustration and the loose end of the tape flaps.

Tabitha reaches through the bars and slaps the tape back down.

My small amount of breathing space disappears.

I'm crushed by the loss.

"Stop being such a baby," Tabitha says. "I thought you were this tough ghost hunter. I thought you were special." She takes out the keyring and the keychains jangle as she turns the lock.

The door swings open with a creak, the greatest sound I've heard.

Seeing the opening, I try to roll out. Rough hands grab my hair. "No funny business. I still have my knife," Tabitha growls as she drops me on the carpet. I stretch my legs and try to wiggle my fingers. The stretching feels amazing. The pins and needles in my hands jab painfully.

Kimmie crouches next to me. "Just about ready for you. You excited?"

Why does she keep asking me that? Why would I want this?

I shake my head and plead with my eyes. Of the two, Kimmie seems like the least crazy.

"Don't look to me for help. I'm loving this." She stands and joins Tabitha at the altar. Candles are lit and chants are said. At one point, Tabitha reads out of the book that looks identical to the book I gave Ford.

Kimmie holds up a coin like Celeste had, and Tabitha holds up one like Marie had.

"Imbue these coins with all the powers of the world, both this side and the side beyond. Let the powers bring back the poor departed soul."

The rapt faces of the girls are terrifying. The whole scene could be from a bad movie, but they believe it completely. Believe so much that they've committed murder.

I look at the rotting woman on the floor next to me. Why would they want to bring her back? Would her soul take this decomposed form?

If I haven't seen the things I have, I would laugh at such an idea. But I am well versed in things beyond the dead.

What if this is real?

I look around the room for anything that might help me escape. Besides the altar, the room is full of shelves of books and scary-looking statues. I have stared at this room for hours and there is nothing to help me. Especially with my hands taped.

The girls finish their incantations, then crouch next to me.

"It's time," Kimmie says enthusiastically.

"To the tree out back," Tabitha says, pulling on my arm to pick me up. "We have everything ready for you."

They roughly carry me down the stairs and out the back door. The full moon is out and I can see the backyard of tall weeds and a few trees. Beyond the trees are rusting hulks of forgotten cars and trucks. We pass the old vehicles, silent witnesses to the horror to be inflicted on me. Just beyond is a large tree with a yellow rope at the base. The same kind of rope used on Celeste and Marie.

A fire crackles nearby.

The fire is meant for me.

When I see it, I buck and kick, fight as best I can.

They lose their grip and I fall to the ground. I land on my side, my face in the weeds. All I can see is green and shadows.

I want to stay here on the ground. I want to be anywhere but tied to that tree.

"Stupid," Tabitha shouts and kicks me in the ribs.

I squeal in pain.

They each grab an arm and drag me toward the tree. I'm soon on my feet, leaning against the trunk. The bark digs into my hands behind my back. Kimmie pushes on my chest, holding me in place, as Tabitha begins looping the yellow rope around me and the tree.

I lunge forward, but Kimmie pushes me. "You're not going anywhere."

I'm frantic and beg her with my eyes, try to talk into the tape.

Kimmie laughs, a horrible sound. "You should see your face right now."

Tabitha comes around the tree and looks, then laughs as well. "Priceless. Celeste and Marie weren't scared. They were excited to be part of something so amazing. Of course they didn't understand what was coming. This fear is much better."

My legs grow weak and the ropes hold me up. I don't see a way out. I think of my dad and how devastated he will be to lose me.

I think of Keaton and how this will hurt him.

I think of Val and Mickey and their pain.

I think of Mom's ghost locked in my house with no one to know she is there.

I even think of George and how he has been stuck in my bathroom all day.

Then I think of Ford and the fact that he will never know how I feel about him.

As the ropes tighten, I lean my head back against the tree and pray.

"God, please let me live. If I can't live, please take me to you."

My greatest fear is being stuck like mom. I don't want to be part of this world and the next but not part of either.

The girls are chanting now, walking in circles around the tree, holding the coins in the air. The fire is so close, I can feel its warmth, but it isn't burning me.

Not yet.

I am helpless.

They stop in front of me and Tabitha tears the tape from my mouth. I gasp in pain and take in the precious air.

"I don't volunteer," I say, as soon as I catch my breath. "You need me to volunteer for this and I don't. This is against my will."

"Shut up," Tabitha says and takes the knife from her pocket. She opens the blade and presses it to my shoulder.

"The blood will bring her back," she chants.

The blade slices into my skin and I shout in pain. Tabitha takes the knife away and looks at the blood on the blade. She smiles.

And I begin to lose faith.

She cuts me again, this time on the other shoulder. Kimmie watches, rapt with excitement.

"My turn," she says and takes the knife.

She slices through my jeans, then cuts my thigh. The pain is horrible, but I almost welcome it. As long as I feel, I am alive.

They continue cutting and I clench my teeth, not willing to give them the satisfaction of hearing me cry.

They grow more excited with each slice. Taking turns running the blade in short swipes on my skin.

I begin to grow weak with the pain all over my body. I imagine shadows surrounding the tree.

Tabitha stops cutting me and picks up a branch that is half in the nearby fire. Flames flicker on the end.

"Now, we just need you to volunteer." She holds the flame close to my arm, so close the hair singes. I try to pull away, but the ropes hold me in place.

"Say you volunteer and the fire is gone," she hisses.

"I don't volunteer," I repeat, again and again. "I don't volunteer!"

One of the shadows I thought was my delusional imagination takes shape.

"She doesn't volunteer," the ghost of Tabitha's mother says.

Tabitha drops the burning branch.

To my surprise, both girls look at the ghost.

They can see her.

TWENTY-NINE

FORD PIERCE

I don't tell Tyler what I saw at Tabitha's house. I'm not even sure what it was. A shadow? Is that how Rylan sees what she sees, as a shadow?

When we return to the precinct, I keep thinking of Rylan. I want to tell her about what I saw. I know Tabitha is hiding something. Maybe the ghost is trying to communicate.

I need Rylan to help me with this.

"I'm going out for some air," I tell Tyler when the urge to call her gets so strong I can't ignore it. Rylan could help with the case.

"Okay," he says, not looking up from his desk.

I step out of the lobby into the front entrance and the fading light and take out my phone. My finger hovers over the call button. What am I going to tell her? After last night, will she even take my call?

I guess not, because Rylan doesn't answer.

After getting so worked up over whether or not to call her, the voicemail is disheartening.

I stare at the rising moon, tinged with pink from the setting sun on the opposite horizon. It is lovely.

But my mind is in turmoil.

Wrong. Something feels wrong.

"Hey, Ford," a female voice calls from the sidewalk.

It's Mickey Ramirez. My stomach sinks further.

"Hey, Mickey. Everything okay?"

"I came here looking for you. I think something might be wrong with Rylan."

My heart skips a beat. She's saying the words I was thinking.

"Why's that?"

She looks at the ground. "I'm sure I'm just being paranoid, but with everything going on with her aunt and all."

"What's happened?"

"Nothing's happened. It's just, she didn't show up to work on the show today and I can't get her on the phone. At first, I didn't think much of it, but it's been hours."

"I just called her and she didn't answer."

Mickey seems surprised. "That's weird, isn't it? What could she be doing all day that she is ducking both of us and not coming to work?"

My mind races, thinks of the ghost motioning me to the stairs.

"Mickey, do you ever see the ghosts?"

She seems startled by the question. "No. But Rylan sees them. I wholeheartedly believe that," she replies, defensive.

"I believe her, too," I assure her. "I just..." I run a hand over my head. "I thought I saw something today at an old farmhouse."

She grows interested. "What was it?"

"I'm not sure. It was just a shadowy shape. But it was motioning me to the top of the stairs. I felt like it wanted me to follow."

"Did you?"

"Of course not. We were talking to a girl in connection with the murders. I couldn't go snooping around her house without permission, and she definitely didn't want to give me free rein of her house. She basically kicked us out."

Mickey looks thoughtful, then says, "What would Rylan do?"

I give a small laugh. "Rylan would have stormed up the steps to see what was going on."

"Exactly."

"Exactly what?"

"I can't see what she sees, but I've learned to trust her instincts. If your instinct is that something is going on in that house, you need to find out."

I'm suddenly anxious to return to Tabitha Lipinsky's. Right now. "Thank you," I say to Mickey. "I'll let you know what I find out."

Mickey follows me a few steps, pulls on my sleeve. "Let me come with you. I might be able to help."

"What would Rylan tell you?"

"She'd say stay behind the camera," she says, sounding defeated, but she stops following me.

I leave her behind and hurry to my personal car. I don't want Tyler to come with me on what is probably a wild goose chase. What am I supposed to tell him, that I saw a ghost and I'm going to try to talk to it?

He might believe in Rylan's abilities, but that only goes so far. If I start chasing after ghosts, he'll turn me in for losing my mind.

I drive to Tabitha's as quickly as I can, dread growing with every mile. I try Rylan's phone again but get no answer. Soon, I'm pulling into the long, weed-choked driveway.

The house is mostly dark when I park. A wavering light is in an upstairs bedroom window. A candle maybe?

The same car that was here before is parked out front. Tabitha should be home.

I climb the porch steps and beat on the front door, a loud pounding that can't be ignored.

The house is silent as a tomb.

I beat on the door again, adrenaline pumping. "Tabitha, are you in there?"

No answer.

I try the door handle and it turns.

Do I go in?

Rylan is missing, I don't care.

I push the door open and enter the house.

I search each room on the ground floor quickly, then, with my flashlight guiding the way, I hurry up the stairs. One of the doors on the hall is open, a dim light falling onto the red flowered carpet.

"Hello?" I call.

The candlelight wavers.

I put my back against the hall wall and take out my gun. Then I notice the smell. The smell of death. It is strong here, and I brace myself for what I may see.

I quickly turn and point my gun into the room.

There is no one there.

At least no one alive.

The rotting corpse, which I guess to be Agatha Lipinsky, lies on the floor, surrounded by half-thawed two-liter bottles of ice.

I've seen dead bodies in all sorts of states, but never one that has been left on purpose like this. I do a quick check of the body. Its neck is turned at an unnatural angle, the likely cause of death.

I spin in a slow circle, taking in the dark altar with the burning candles. There's a book, identical to the one Rylan gave me, open to the page with the victim tied to a tree.

Then I see the cage.

I approach slowly. When I'm next to the cage, I can see a

wet spot in the carpet beneath the bars of the floor. It smells like urine, even above the smell of the corpse. Someone has been in this cage recently.

I pray it wasn't Rylan.

Was that what the ghost wanted me to see?

Was Rylan in this cage when I was here earlier?

The thought makes me sick.

But where is she now?

I hurry into the hall, then check the other rooms. They are all empty.

That's when I hear her.

"I don't volunteer."

It's Rylan.

I run into a bedroom and look out the back window. I see her in the moonlight.

A familiar scene.

She's tied to a tree just like in the crime scenes.

I run down the hall, calling for backup as I go.

THIRTY

RYLAN FLYNN

"This will never work," the ghost tells the girls. "You have this wrong. She needs to volunteer. You tied her and put her in the cage. Is that volunteering?"

The girls cower from the ghost. "But, Mom, I'm just doing what you said," Tabitha tries.

"I never said anything like this."

"You wanted blood," Tabitha says.

"You wanted us to bring you back," Kimmie says.

"I said no such thing. And this will never work, you stupid girls." The ghost flies at them, and they cower away. "Cut her down."

"But I'm doing this for you," Tabitha cries. "To bring you back like you said."

The ghost seems disgusted. "Like I said? I'm dead upstairs right now and can't say anything." Her face grows angry. "Thanks for pushing me down the stairs, by the way," she adds with heavy sarcasm.

Tabitha cowers on her knees. "It was an accident. I promise."

The ghost laughs. "That's what you always said. When our cat went missing and I found it without its eyes, you said that."

"It was," Tabitha says miserably. "I didn't mean to do it."

"And you didn't mean to kidnap this woman?"

"We had to," Kimmie says. "She has special powers. She's the best one to bring your soul back."

The ghost turns on Kimmie. "And you? I always knew you were trouble."

Kimmie lifts her chin and stares the ghost in the face. "I'm not trouble."

"Ha. Now you girls stop playing with things you don't understand and cut her down."

Tabitha does as she's asked and I feel the ropes fall away.

"Now cut the tape." The ghost shakes her head. "What were you thinking?"

I rub my wrists once they are freed. I hurt everywhere. I touch the worst of the cuts, through my jeans and on my thigh. My hand comes away, bloody.

The girls are now on their knees, their heads bowed in submission.

"But we were going to do both coins and the fire," Tabitha tries to explain. "We only wanted you to come back." To my surprise, Tabitha sniffles. I wouldn't think she had it in her to feel that deeply. "Don't you want to come back?"

"Not like this. Is this what you learned from all my teaching?" She points at me.

"I'm just, I'm sorry for what I did to you," Tabitha says. "I want to make it right. I thought this was what you wanted."

"Then let her go and take your punishment."

I slowly, slowly move around the tree while they are distracted. I take a chance and sprint into the dark field of abandoned cars.

"She's getting away," Tabitha says. Her feet soon pound the ground in pursuit.

My legs are weak from being tied all day and then being sliced. I run as hard as I can, but she's gaining on me.

At the edge of my consciousness, I think I hear Ford saying, "Police. Get down on the ground."

I know he can't be there, so I don't turn to look. I run between two trucks rotting away in the moonlit weeds.

I try the first door and it opens. I climb inside the truck, the wire springs of the rotted front seat poking my already stinging skin.

"Rylan Flynn," Tabitha singsongs, "Where are you?"

I can see her through the dirty windshield, searching for me. The knife in her hand flashes in the moonlight.

"Come back, Rylan. We aren't done with you, no matter what Mom says. We must try. We didn't even get to the coins or the fire yet."

Thank God.

She's so close, I can barely breathe. One of the seat's springs is especially painful, poking into my back. I shift slightly.

Tabitha sees the tiny movement.

"There you are!" She hurries to the side of the truck.

The door to the truck is ajar a few inches. I kick it and it slams open into Tabitha, tossing her against the truck next to us.

She slides to the ground with a satisfying "*umph.*"

I climb out of the truck and run toward the house.

Out of the corner of my eye, I see Ford chasing Kimmie into the field of cars. He really is here. But Kimmie seems to be outpacing him. She's surprisingly fast.

I'm not as fast, and I feel Tabitha gaining on me as I pound up the back steps into the house. I don't know where to go, but I keep running. When I see the stairway, I run up them as fast as I can.

Tabitha almost catches me by the ankle, but I shake her off. Agatha stands at the top of the steps. I dart around her and into the ritual room.

"Mom, she's getting away," Tabitha shouts at the ghost. "We need her."

"It's over, Tabitha." I listen from behind the door.

"Why aren't you helping me?" Tabitha wails. "This is all for you."

"I didn't want any of this. I didn't want to be killed or for that to lead to more murder."

"You're the one that told me to do it all. Your painting told me."

"Stop talking nonsense. Now you've been bad, Tabitha. You know what you need to do."

"Not the cage," she begs.

"You brought this on yourself."

To my surprise, Tabitha marches into the room. She steps around the dead body and goes to the cage.

"But it's wet in here," she says.

"Get in."

She drops to her knees and climbs inside.

The door slams shut and the lock turns.

Tabitha sees me cowering behind the door. She looks me straight in the eye, then reaches through the bars.

It takes me a moment to understand what she's doing. The cage is next to the altar and she reaches for a lit candle. She moves the candle to the nearby window.

Seeing what she's about to do, I jump over the body and try to grab the candle.

I'm too late. The curtains go up in flame, faster than I would have imagined. I pull one down and put it out. I attempt to grab the other, but it is too far gone. The flames are climbing across the old wallpaper now.

"Let her out," I beg Agatha.

She stands like a statue. "She did this to herself. The fire will purify her."

"The fire will kill her." The flames are crawling across the wall, reaching toward the ceiling. Smoke burns my throat, makes me cough.

"I will be with you soon, Mom," Tabitha says.

I can't let her sit here and burn. I grab the cage bars and pull. The cage moves a few inches.

"Leave me alone," she yells hitting my fingers.

"I won't let you kill yourself like this." I pull again and the cage drags another few inches. I cough and pull again.

Suddenly, strong hands are next to mine on the bars.

Ford is here. "Pull," he says.

Together, the cage moves much easier. "Unlock this cage," I beg Agatha. "She's your daughter. Don't let her do this."

"I can't," Agatha says defiantly.

"Yes you can. You locked it. Now unlock the door."

She tilts her already cocked head and the door to the cage swings open.

Ford is surprised, but quickly recovers. He reaches into the cage and pulls Tabitha out. She tries to hold onto the bars.

"Let me die. I failed. I deserve this."

He picks her up easily and tosses her over his shoulder. "Let's get out of here," he says, and ushers me out of the heat and smoke.

We hurry down the steps and into the night air. In the distance, sirens sing.

Ford drops Tabitha on the ground. He sits her up and puts cuffs on her. "Don't move," he says. She lies there in a heap, crying. She's not going anywhere.

Ford helps her to her feet, then puts her in the car's backseat next to Kimmie.

He calls for a fire truck in addition to the police he already called, then turns to me.

"What in the world just happened? Who were you talking to?"

"The ghost of Agatha Lipinsky. She's the one that locked Tabitha in the cage."

Ford seems thoughtful, but accepts my explanation. "How did the fire start?"

"Tabitha lit it with a candle. I tried to put it out, but the curtains just took off."

We look at the house, the flames filling the upstairs windows. In one of them, I see a figure. Agatha's ghost stares down at us as flames burn behind her. I wonder if that's how she'll spend eternity, with flames around her.

We watch the house burning, helpless to stop it. The heat from the fire warms my face. As the flames grow, we have to step back into the trees.

That's when I see another figure in the side yard.

It's Marie, beautiful and bloody.

"Give me a minute," I tell Ford, then walk toward the ghost.

She's close to the house, so close I can feel the heat of the fire.

"It's okay," I say with my hands held wide. "I won't hurt you. I know you are scared."

She cowers a little then takes a step toward me. A hissing sound escapes the wound in her neck.

"I can help you go home," I tell her. I think of what Dad would do in this situation. "Would you pray with me?"

She nods.

"Lord, please take this soul back to you. Please welcome her home." Behind her, a light opens in the darkness, brighter than the moon. Brighter than the fire burning nearby.

I repeat the prayer, and the light grows larger, seems to fill the sky.

Marie looks at it, then back to me, her face full of questions. "Just step into it," I say gently, coaxing. "You're going home, Marie."

She turns to the light, looks over her shoulder. "Thank you," she mouths.

Then the light is gone, and so is she.

Ford walks up beside me. "I saw a light," he says in a low voice.

"You did? That was God. He took Marie home."

He pats me on the shoulder. "It was beautiful." The pat sends tingles down my arm, but also stings the cut there.

"Are you okay?" he asks. "You're covered in blood."

I look at my sliced and bloody body. I do a mental check. "I think I'm okay. Cut, but not hurt badly."

"I'll call an ambulance."

"No need." I rub a hand over my cut arms, blood stains my palms.

"You sure?"

"I'm sure." I touch the deepest of the cuts on my thigh and flinch. "On second thought, maybe a hospital is a good idea. I really hurt." I sit in the grass, shaking with shock and unable to stand.

Ford crouches and looks my cuts over. "A few of these might need stitches."

"Why are you here?" I ask in wonder. "How did you know to come?"

He looks over the field. "Does it matter?"

I can tell he's hiding something, but I let him keep his secret. It's only fair. I rarely tell him the whole truth either. "I guess not. I'm just glad you came." I climb to my feet. I'm so shaky, I lose my balance and fall into his strong arms.

I let myself enjoy the almost embrace a moment before I regain my balance.

"Ambulance for sure," he says, steadying me.

Did his arms just tighten around me?

I must be woozier than I thought.

THIRTY-ONE

VAL FLYNN

The metal bench presses uncomfortably into my rear. I shift to find a more comfortable position, but there is no comfort in this jail cell.

I need to use the restroom again, but I don't want to. The metal bowl in the middle of the room is not something I want to visit until absolutely necessary again.

I can wait.

I squirm and keep my head down. So far, I've avoided confrontation from the other women here. I'd like to keep it that way.

The jingle of keys carries down the hall toward the metal bars of the holding cell. I raise my eyes and look at the officer's approach.

"Flynn," he says, searching the faces around me.

I slowly rise to my feet. "That's me," I say, full of trepidation.

"You're being released."

My knees grow weak and nearly buckle with relief.

"I'm going home?"

"Looks like it." He puts the key into the lock and it clicks open. The greatest sound I've ever heard.

I don't waste time. I hurry out the door as soon as it opens.

"What happened?" I ask.

"They found the killers."

"Killers? As in plural?"

The officer shrugs. "Looks like it."

I follow his steps, too slow for my taste. They process me and send me out the door to Keaton, who is waiting in the lobby.

"Aunt Val," he says, and wraps me in his arms.

"What's going on? What happened to make them change their mind?"

"Rylan happened."

He tells me about how Rylan was kidnapped and tortured, and how Kimmie and Tabitha were the killers.

"Kimmie from work?" I ask in disbelief as we climb into his car. "I can't imagine."

"Believe it. They were caught red-handed trying to do the same thing to Rylan."

"Is she okay?"

"Rylan? She's cut and battered a bit, but she's okay. They took her to the hospital."

"I want to see her."

The door to Rylan's hospital room in the ER is closed. I look through the tiny window and see her on the bed, resting.

I push the door open slowly, Keaton behind me.

"Hey," I say as she opens her eyes.

She sits up quickly and reaches for me. "Val, you're free," she exclaims.

"Thanks to you," I say, folding her into my arms.

"Yeah, that." She sits back in the hospital bed.

I look over her injuries, the many bandages. "They really cut you, didn't they?"

Her eyes are a bit soft, her smile wavering. "I don't feel too much. They gave me some good pain meds." She finally sees her brother. "Keaton, you came."

He looks uncomfortable. "Had to make sure you were okay." He looks to the wall behind her, to the floor. Anywhere but at his bandaged sister. "Look, I should get home to Sheryl." He slips out the door after patting her awkwardly on the shoulder.

Rylan watches the door close behind him, then reaches for my hand.

"I'm so sorry, Val," Rylan says, her voice slurred from the medication. "I can't imagine what you've been through."

"Don't worry about that now. Just rest."

Rylan lays back on her pillow and closes her eyes. "He saved me," she murmurs, then drifts to sleep.

I'm not sure who the "he" is, but I imagine she's talking about Ford.

Will he come see her? What will I do when I see him again?

I hold her hand while she sleeps, praying for direction.

Can I forgive Ford Pierce for locking me up?

It isn't long until I must find out. The door opens again.

I go still when I see Ford.

He looks around the room, his eyes lingering on me a long moment. He nods, then turns to Rylan.

"How's she doing?" he asks.

"She should get to go home soon," I tell him.

We stand, awkward in the quiet. Rylan's monitor beeps softly.

"Look, Val, I'm so sorry," Ford says, his face pleading.

I want to hold a grudge. I want to blame him.

Only Kimmie and Tabitha are to blame.

I know what must be done. "I understand you had good evidence against me."

"We did. We really did. I know it probably doesn't matter, but I never actually believed you were capable of that."

"Well, that's something," I say sarcastically.

"I know you're upset, and you have every right to be. I can only ask to be forgiven."

"Fine. Ford Pierce, I forgive you."

Tension falls from his shoulders. "Thank you." He shuffles his feet. "I'm not proud of how this all went, but I'm glad you're here now."

I look at a sleeping Rylan and agree. "Me too."

"I should leave you with her." He turns toward the door. He looks longingly over his shoulder to the bed, his emotions raw. He hesitates, then feels me studying him. His hand on the door, he looks at me sheepishly. "You'll tell her I came?"

"I'll let her know."

Another glance at a sleeping Rylan and he is gone.

I'm surprised to find myself smiling.

THIRTY-TWO

RYLAN FLYNN

Seventeen stitches and many hours later, I'm released from the hospital and I can go home to let George out. He gets to go home.

Once taken into custody, Kimmie spilled the whole story. Ford said, later, that Tabitha sulked and refused to make a statement beyond, "You should have left me there in the cage."

Turns out Celeste didn't know she was in danger and, as we thought, her choking on the coin was an accident.

Marie volunteered because she didn't know what Tabitha had planned. Kimmie said that when Tabitha cut Marie's throat, she was afraid. She went along with Tabitha's plans to stay safe.

I know firsthand that she enjoyed it, that she was a willing partner.

That two young girls could be so evil still makes my skin crawl.

Tabitha said it was Kimmie's idea to frame Val by putting a bloody knife in her house. Of course, Kimmie denied it. In the end they just pointed fingers at each other. In their efforts to frame the other, they provided the DA's office with plenty of evidence to convict them both.

The next day, Val, Dad, Mickey, Keaton, and I all meet at The Hole for a celebration of sorts. Mostly, I want to see everyone after almost losing them all. They were only too eager to come.

We eat donuts and drink coffee and enjoy the fact that I'm alive and Val is free.

Eileen is at The Hole as usual. She can't stop apologizing for leaving me alone and waiting in the long line at the post office.

"It's not your fault," I tell her again as she wipes down the counter. "The girls would have taken me from wherever they found me."

"But I should have called the police when you weren't here when I got back."

"You had no way of knowing I was kidnapped," I assure her. "Please don't feel bad."

Eileen looks up from the counter as someone comes in the door.

It's Ford.

My heart skips a beat seeing him.

I scoot over and he sits next to me in the booth.

"Thank you so much for saving our Rylan," Dad says.

"She kind of saved herself," Ford says, looking at me out of the corner of his eye.

"You're just saying that," I say, off-center with him so close. I can feel the heat of his thigh against my stitched up one.

"So, you going to stay out of trouble now?" Keaton asks, too serious for my taste.

"Why would I do that?" I tease, trying to keep the mood light.

"We have shows to film," Mickey says.

"And souls to help," I add. I think of the Morton Mistress stuck in the abandoned hospital. I think of the little girl Sarah wandering around the cemetery.

The thing in Keaton's room flashes through my mind, but I push it away. My ability to help has a limit.

"Yes, we have work to do," Dad says, reaching across the table to squeeze my hand.

"As long as you don't get involved in another murder," Keaton says.

"I second that," Ford says.

I want to defend myself, but am interrupted by Eileen. "Can I help you?" Eileen says to a woman that walked into the shop. The woman seems flustered, agitated, her eyes darting around the room.

"I'm looking for—oh, there he is."

Any good feelings I had disappear in that moment.

The woman in the shop is the same woman that almost stole everything from my future.

Ford's ex-fiancé, Kaitlyn Freeman.

"Ford, I need your help."

He stiffens. I can't tell if it's because he's angry at seeing her or excited.

"What's wrong?" he asks.

"My cousin, Bess Freeman, is missing. I need you to find her." Kaitlyn holds out a picture.

I can't help but look at it.

I recognize the smiling face with the deep dimple.

Not because I know Kaitlyn's cousin.

I recognize her as the woman with the long braid that ran into me as I entered The Lock Up the other night.

I pull in a breath and Kaitlyn looks at me.

"Do you know her?"

"When did she disappear?" I ask.

"She went to The Lock Up to watch Loose Gravel play Friday night. No one has seen her since."

With a sinking feeling, I realize I was the last one to see Bess Freeman.

And I saw the man she left with.

A LETTER FROM DAWN

Dearest reader,

A huge thank you for choosing to read *The Spirit Girls*. I truly appreciate you. I hope you loved it. If you did enjoy it, and want to keep up to date with all my latest releases, just sign up at the following link. Your email address will never be shared and you can unsubscribe at any time.

www.secondskybooks.com/dawn-merriman

The Spirit Girls was a ton of fun to write. Rylan's character kept me on my toes. Sometimes characters tend to take over the storyline and head in their own direction despite the best of outlines. Rylan certainly liked to lead me. Following her has been a great ride. I hope you love her as much as I do.

If you enjoyed *The Spirit Girls*, I would be very grateful if you could leave a review. Feedback from writers is so special. I'd love to hear what you think, and it makes such a difference helping new readers to discover one of my books for the first time.

I love hearing from my readers and I interact on my Fan Club on Facebook at the link below. Join the club today and get behind the scenes info on my works, fun games, and interesting tidbits from my life.

Again, thank you for reading *The Spirit Girls*.

Happy reading and God bless,

Dawn Merriman

www.dawnmerriman.com

facebook.com/dawnmerrimannovelist

instagram.com/dawnmerrimannovelist

ACKNOWLEDGMENTS

Writers spend a lot of time alone typing, but this book would not be possible without help from "my team."

First, I'd like to thank my husband, Kevin. He listened tirelessly to me discussing the ins and outs of the story as it progressed. Discussions with him about a sticky plot point often led to a new idea or direction for Rylan. His unwavering support of my career lifts me up.

To my beta reader team, Carlie Frech, Belinda Martin, Katie Hoffman, Jamie Miller and Robin Moyer, the positive influence your early feedback had on *The Spirit Girls* cannot be measured. Thank you for taking the time to read the rough pages and offer insights.

A huge thank you to Bookouture and the wonderful team there. You took a chance on me and Rylan and I will be eternally grateful. My editor, Jack Renninson, has been a wonderful guide through the whole process. Jack, thank you for all the time and effort you have put into *The Spirit Girls* and for believing in my writing.

Thank you to my readers for choosing my stories to spend time with.

Most of all, thank you to God for giving me the gift to tell the stories. I hope I do them justice.

Thank you all,

Dawn Merriman

CPSIA information can be obtained
at www.ICGtesting.com
Printed in the USA
JSHW081249190423
40474JS00006B/180

9 781837 904037